AF392872

DRUG PARADISE

K. Kimuyu

Don't forget the star
The star that shines within you
The star you've always been
- To my sisters

PROLOGUE

The Ghost

AGE HAD STARTED catching up with him. His hair had wisps of silver but his stature was upright. His gait had a swagger and confidence to it that suggested he could be more than he was letting on. In another life, he might have been an athlete or a soldier but in this one, he was a supermarket attendant.

"Find it on aisle twelve, three aisles from the one we are on," he mouthed politely to a customer.

Customers who frequented the supermarket warmed up to him. Fridah was now saying hello—a young mother who was coming to terms with the fact that taking care of a baby was more than posting its pictures on Instagram.

"How are you, Fridah, I hope the baby is well?"

"She's doing much better now. The fever has reduced."

"That's great to hear. Make some mashed pumpkin for her. They are just fresh from the farm. Aisle fifteen."

He moved to aisle ten. His steps silent, as if he were floating and not walking. He stopped to move some tissue-paper boxes. Mark grinned from behind a huge box. His teeth yellow and browning.

Mark was their courier boy. A short, plump guy in his late twenties who always smelt of cigarette smoke.

"How is that migraine going?"

"It's just as bad as yesterday."

"Keep off the cigs and stay busy. The addiction will ebb, eventually."

Many people who interacted with him considered him a darling. In their eyes, he was the type of person who couldn't harm a fly. The type who couldn't break an egg if he jumped on it. He wore a face that you could ask directions from if you were lost; the kind of face that you didn't feel intimidated to walk up to and ask for a soft loan.

If you asked the people around him who he was, they would have told you that he was Charles. The happy-go-lucky guy who was always ready with a smile and a helping hand. A neighborhood friend of good cheer. But they didn't know anything about him besides the veneer he allowed them to see.

He smiled as he entered the kitchenette in the corner of the supermarket. He turned the lock and closed the door behind him as if it were made of clouds—not even a creaking sound was heard. He stared at the board. He had made employee of the month for the third month running. He made a mental note to tone it down a notch. He didn't need a ruckus around him. What he needed was to keep a low profile and be who he had always been. A Ghost.

PART ONE

"Is love a tender thing? It is too rough, too rude, too boisterous and it pricks like thorn. – Romeo, Romeo and Juliet

CHAPTER 1

The Couple

HE WAS A MAN in his mid-thirties and at the peak of his career, with a beautiful fiancée to garnish the entire look, yet there was an aspect of loneliness about him. He stabbed his cigarette on the rim of the iron bar at the balcony, threw the butt in the waste bucket, and heaved a sigh.

It was almost dusk at the Sand Resort in Mombasa. The sun was going down, creating that spectacular, alluring paste that resembled Pablo Picasso playing with a brush.

"Honey, aren't you going to join us?" a soft voice whispered from behind him.

"I will be there in a minute."

"What is more important out here than your engagement party?"

He stared at the ocean. The waves were rising in huge mountains and crashing into each other like gladiators.

In the far distance, a little boy was running with his kite but the wind was too strong and it snatched the kite away. The little boy ran after it and disappeared into the horizon.

"The sunset. Don't you think it's beautiful?"

Lily moved from the door to where her fiancé was.

"More beautiful than your wife?"

She was in a purple evening gown with an empire waist that fell from her tiny waist onto her wide hips like a bell, giving her a fairy tale princess look. It was strapless, revealing her soft shoulders and collarbones. Collarbones that were moody. Sometimes they appeared soft and delicate, other times they were as sharp as an axe.

Resting on the apex of those shoulders was a soft, oval face with spaced out eyes, a duchess nose, and full lips. She had an uncanny look to her. She looked both like a woman who could pass as a business mogul and one who could pose on the cover of a lingerie magazine as a spicy mistress.

"Come," she took his hand. "The guests are getting worried. They want to see you hand in hand with your wife."

"Wife-to-be," he muttered under his breath.

CHAPTER 2

The Best Man

OYUNGA SCANNED THE BALLROOM. It was all an act. It was a big movie scene and every character had their notes. The guests holding their martinis and neat whiskies, chattering. Women in their short dresses. Some married, others there to make sure their husbands didn't stray. Bachelors in bespoke suits and designer watches darting their eyes around, looking for something to warm their beds for the night. Waitresses arching their backs almost to the point of breaking them and flirting with faces bright with smiles, perhaps to woo the young bachelors or perhaps to get better tips.

"Oyunga, where have you been? Everybody is waiting for the man of the moment." Arigula flashed a smile and punched his friend on the arm with a soft fist. "You've decided to leave bachelorhood, eh? I'll tell you this, it better be something your heart wants because this is no bed of roses, my man."

Arigula's wife, June was now craning her neck, wondering where her husband had gone. She was a short woman whose height was only rivaled by her temper, which was even shorter.

"I think you've got bigger fish to fry than the end of my bachelorhood, my friend," Oyunga chirped as the tiny, little thing tottered to where they were and nudged Arigula's arm.

"I was worried sick," she barked. "Don't do that again," she continued as if scolding an errant child.

She was not completely at fault; she had reason to worry. Arigula had had his fair share of infidelities in Nairobi and they were now in Mombasa. The natives called it 'Mombasa Raha.' Girls in tiny garments that made them look more naked than dressed were in plenty. She had a mind to make sure her husband was not sampling anything that wasn't home-cooked.

"Darling, I'm here beside you where I have always been," Arigula said, trying to calm the storm.

"Sorry for barging in like this. I'm sure you understand that a woman in love is a dangerous thing?" June shot, her husband's words having fizzled to wind.

"It's okay, June. A woman in love is a beautiful thing."

"Congratulations to both you and Lily. You make a damn sweet couple. If it got any sweeter, I'd have diabetes," Arigula jumped in and his wife swatted his arm.

"Stop it!" she whispered but both Oyunga and Lily heard and Arigula lowered his head, embarrassed.

"Thank you, Arigula," Lily said with a half-smile and tapped him on the shoulder to help him save face.

"Nice meeting you," June said, pulling her husband away by the arm like a warden pulling her inmate.

CHAPTER 3

Prisca

"Oh my god! Oh my God!"

Prisca penguin-ran in her Burj Khalifa high heels and clubby, tight, yellow dress towards Lily and embraced her tightly, almost breaking her frame.

"I can't believe you're getting married." She pulled her away from Oyunga, held both of Lily's hands in hers, and brushed her eyes over her as if seeing her for the first time, then broke out again, this time her feet doing a small jig as if she badly needed to pee. "Oh my God! Oh my God!"

Lily stretched her arm out, almost dislocating her shoulder, to flaunt her engagement bling which sparkled like a shooting star. "Eighteen-carat diamond. He got it for me in Dubai." Of course the story kept being tweaked depending on whom she was talking to.

"Oyunga, you lucky, lucky son of a gun. *Ulijinyakulia rangi ya thao*, top layer, eh?" Prisca chortled in a coastal accent.

"*Huyu hapa hurulaini.*"

Oyunga blushed. "*Asante.*"

"Oh my God! I forgot. Meet my other friend, Marion. She's in advertising. Lily, this is Marion, Marion–Lily. Oyunga, this is Marion. Marion–Oyunga."

If at that moment you had told Prisca that that introduction would be Lily's and Oyunga's undoing, she would have smacked you in the face with her heels and called you crazy.

Marion stood awe-stricken by her friend's energy. She had never quite gotten used to it. She lifted her eyes shyly and they locked with Oyunga's. She felt as if his brown eyes were searing right through her, unbuttoning her. She froze momentarily, the magnetic spark making her tipsy. She steadied herself and looked away, reminding herself that he was an engaged man, a man who was out of bounds. She gave both of them a soft hug, knowing she couldn't hang around, scared of what would happen if the spark gripped her again.

"Congratulations, you two. It is a pleasure. Prisca has told me a lot about you and I'm glad she was not exaggerating on the picture-perfect bit."

"Thank you," Lily said, her face impassive, as if she were seated in a casino playing poker. Oyunga was glad that Lily was the one who responded. He felt that if he were the one who did, he would have gone the extra mile and added a, "You look quite dashing yourself," on top of the thank you.

She did look dashing. She was in a white, off-shoulder skater dress and black heels, which she complemented with a pearl necklace and cream chandelier earrings. She looked like Lupita Nyong'o. Her hair was trimmed short and she had an angelic face. The kind of face that was attractive regardless of whether it was sad or happy.

"I will stretch my legs and let the couple enjoy themselves. Au revoir!" And damn were they beautiful legs. Long and sexy. Flowing on and on like a river of chocolate.

CHAPTER 4

The Couple

THEY WALKED AROUND the room doing the ritual that many people faked so well. Grinning just enough to convince people that they were genuinely happy. Shaking people's hands firmly and patting them on the back when they went in for a hug to assure them they were inviting.

The questions kept coming. Oyunga found them dull and tedious. One, in particular, kept being repeated. "How did you guys meet?" someone would ask and Lily would go into her act. Lowering her head at first as if she were shy and adjusting her tone to set the scene to something out of a romance novel. If she had her way she would have had violins and pianos humming softly in the background.

"We met in Dubai's underwater zoo. I was marveling at the sheer size of the aquarium when I saw this shark approaching me, only it was a tall, sculpted shark that looked as if it lived in the gym."

"He was in a suit, his beard unshaven, and he looked at me with those smoldering, brown eyes that unzipped me and for a moment my legs almost buckled. What is it you say attracted you to me again, hon?"

"Your large hazelnut eyes. They were so kind. They had this spark about them that I just couldn't resist."

"He couldn't stop calling me after that. You know, I thought he was one of those guys who just wanted to get into my panties so I ignored him for a while but he just kept charging at me like a bull. As if I were a bullfighter holding a muleta."

"What can I say, I'm a persistent guy."

"Yes, romantic too. I can't start telling you the number of times he sent me flowers and chocolate. Over and over again and I said yes just so I could avoid cavities."

"Haha. Ladies and gents, there you have it. The way to a woman's heart is not love and affection, it's flowers and chocolate."

What they left out in their choreographed skit was that they met in a seedy restaurant in downtown Nairobi. Oyunga, always the forlorn chap, was having anxiety attacks and the medication he was getting from hospitals wasn't helping. He got a contact from an acquaintance who knew someone who could get him the meds he needed. He ended up getting so addicted to Lily's supply that when he didn't get it, besides anxiety attacks he now got tense and agitated too.

She also left out the part about her dropping her knickers for him that same night after they overdosed on the pills and their inhibitions left them, although Lily would have bedded him with or without the pills because she was that type of girl. The kind of girl that didn't play dating games when she knew all she wanted was carnal pleasure. In that regard, she was a little bit like a man. She loved the pleasure of having sex and could take the emotion out of it. Even now, Oyunga could not tell if she loved him or if it was just another skit.

CHAPTER 5

Marion

MARION FLOUNCED ALONG the corridor, her round behind bobbing up and down in rhythm, her hips rising and falling like a tide. She was in a short, blue, satin skirt, black wedges, and an olive green blouse. On her wrist a simple but elegant Burberry watch. Her Viktor Rolf Flowerbomb fragrance permeated as she entered the boardroom.

They were all waiting for her, the customer service manager in charge of a team of eleven. She made sure that the brands they handled were well satisfied. This, for the most part, included having lunches and sending fruit baskets to the brands' marketing teams. She was in the business of relationships and she understood that business relationships were not built on emails but in person, with love and affection.

She sat in the boardroom and listened to five of her juniors go on a rant about a certain colleague whom they wanted fired because, as they put it, she contributed very little and was always aloof and estranged from the team.

"We had a team-building exercise the other day and she didn't even show up," Wambui's words filled the boardroom.

"Not to mention that we often end up shouldering most of her work," Joshua jumped on the wagon.

"She needs to go," Rehab murmured.

"Who gave you permission to let people go, Rehab?" Marion smirked, staring knives at her. "Team, do you see what is wrong with this picture?"

They all looked clueless.

"You're ganging up on one person. Don't you think that is wrong? The five of you against one, do you think that's a fair fight?" There was a silence, a silence that could sit in the boardroom and help itself to the biscuits that were on the table. "You know what I think, I think you've alienated her and in return, she's alienated you. Call her in here."

Joshua shot out like an arrow, as if there were needles on his chair, and was soon back with Njoki.

"What seems to be the problem, Njoki?" Marion said pulling up a chair for her to sit.

"What is going on?" Njoki said feeling ambushed.

"Your team says you are removed from your job, that you don't engage, and they want to rectify it. See how they can work around it, if not through it." She paused to allow her words to settle. "You're an asset to this company, Njoki, and growth to you is also growth to us."

"Ever since I came here, I have felt like an outcast," Njoki started without preamble. "I don't smoke and the majority, if not all, of the customer service guys here smoke. They will be at the gazebo puffing, huffing, sharing jokes, and gossiping. I'm okay with that but when it comes to work, I'm not even copied on some emails and I'm excluded from meetings and, like an angel, I'm expected to know what is going on and deliver. Is that fair?"

"Josh, Wambui, team, anything you have to add to that?"

"What about the team-building exercise we had? Everybody attended except you. What's your excuse this time, huh?" Wambui shot again.

"Who goes where they're not wanted, or rather, where they don't feel welcome?"

"Enough! Here's what's going to happen," Marion barked. "You're going to copy Njoki on all the emails and you're going to copy me as well. She will also attend all the meetings you attend. And Njoki, you need to open up a bit more. Let people in sometimes. I know you're a little bit of an introvert and if you had your way you would do everything by yourself but you will burn out if you continue like that. This work doesn't end but we do."

"Now get up and shake hands. I want you to start getting along and to stop thinking small. Stop thinking in terms of backbiting and meaningless gossip because that's something I won't entertain. I don't want to walk these corridors and hear things like, 'Njoki has the CS manager in her pocket' or, 'They must be relatives.' You need to think bigger than gossip. You need to think in terms of growth. When you grow, we grow."

Njoki started clapping and the entire room was soon uproarious.

CHAPTER 6

Flowers

MARION SAT IN her office, tapping her biro on the desk, a thousand thoughts racing in her mind. There was a bouquet smack in the middle of her desk that took up almost half of the space. Beside the flowers was a big box of chocolate and a card. She had read the thing a hundred times already.

I know you felt the magnetic spark, I felt it too.

She was ruffled and bent out of shape. She wished that this was another one of her juniors' civil feuds which she knew how to diffuse. But this got her hot under the collar and she didn't understand it. Why would an engaged man send her flowers?

Maybe it's not Oyunga, she thought. *But who else did you have a magnetic spark with recently?*

There was a number on the card. She kept thumbing it. She had memorized it by now.

"Marion."

The CEO, Suthir Sandeep, opened the door without knocking. "Can I see you in my office for a bit?"

She was used to this: the CEO calling her out of nowhere to address frivolous issues. Issues that had no legs. She put on her game face, smoothed her skirt, and catwalked towards the CEO's office.

"How did today's meeting go?" Sandeep asked, his eyes massaging her body. Despite having a wife, he had asked Marion out countless times, and she had declined every time. He respected that but nobody had said he couldn't have his way with her with his two perfectly functioning eyeballs. *Mmh, mhh, mhh, what a meal,* he thought as Marion told him the meeting went on fine. *Fine is what you are, you pretty thing.*

"Sandeep, did you hear me? I said the meeting went on fine."

"Do I need to have a report on the same?" he tried to recover.

"I don't think that will be necessary. It was a minor feud."

"Alright, I don't suppose you will be joining us later today to celebrate the winning of the Unilever account?"

"I will be dropping by momentarily."

"Okay, I will see you then."

She turned and left her boss's eyes having a feast.

CHAPTER 7

The Response

MARION WAS CLUMSY in the kitchen in her Kilimani home. She couldn't seem to do anything right. A sufuria had fallen and she had just burnt her omelet. The flowers Oyunga had bought her sat on her dining table like a bad omen, reminding her of him. She admitted that they were nice flowers. Crimson red roses: the color of passion, romance, and naked lust. She held the kitchen counter with a Samson grip as if she would fall to the floor if she let go.

She had planned out her Saturday. She would have a shower, slip into her pajamas then sit down on the couch to watch an episode of Grey's Anatomy and maybe catch up on a bit of work on her laptop.

She jumped into the shower and decided to make it a cold one. Maybe the cold drops hitting her hot skin would wash away her lewd thoughts.

She toweled and lotioned then sat on the couch with the remote in her hand but she was restless. All she could see was her phone.

She decided to pick it up and fight through it. She thumbed open the Instagram app and clicked on the stories. Someone was talking about how expensive things had gotten, another one was showing images of groceries in the open market, some other person was showing hair tutorials and yet another had a live video but she wasn't talking; all she was doing was throwing two fingers in the air and sticking her tongue out. She wondered how any of these stories were interesting.

She closed Instagram and opened Twitter. She loved Twitter for its newsy and real-time appeal. It was also a great place to source people you wanted to work with as well as have a conversation. But this morning it was full of sexual innuendos. Her timeline was reeking of lust and angst and it didn't help her situation. She closed it and put her phone away, feeling as if the entire world was conspiring to make her cave in.

She went to the kitchen and picked up a bowl of grapes, mixed them with yogurt then sat down and wiped it clean. For a moment, it shut down the need to respond to Oyunga's bouquet and box of chocolates. Chocolates that she had already gourmandized shamelessly. *Should I respond?* The idea kept creeping back into her mind like an unwanted pimple on the face.

She picked up her laptop and scrolled through her emails. Everything seemed okay. She was in the kind of industry where problems erupted when you least expected them to. A client might have hated the artwork, the wrong ad might have aired, a brand might be having over-the-top

expectations, someone in her team might be shutting down…
and she had to stay on top of all of it. There were no off
days in her calendar; she was always on. Twenty-four hours a
day. Seven days a week.

She went to the kitchen again, her phone in hand, and
steadied herself on the counter. She thought of calling her
friend, Prisca, and giggled at the thought of it, imagining
how that conversation would go.

"Remember the couple you introduced me to?"

"Yeah?"

"I think the chap has the hots for me and I'm thinking
of responding to his advances."

Prisca, with her over-the-top personality would probably
scream a thunderstorm. Even though she was in the middle
of planning a wedding. She thought about the groom for
a moment. There was something about him that didn't sit
right. She grinned. *She was the one who didn't sit right.*

*Maybe I will just draft the text. What do I even want to tell him?
Isn't he an engaged man?*

What are you doing? a voice in her head chimed. *Leave it
alone. If you respond you will give it voice.*

But she had already drafted the text and punched in the
number on the card.

*You're an engaged man. Whatever kinds of games you're trying
to play, stop.*

She looked at the text, momentarily telling herself she
couldn't send it, then in a rush of adrenaline, she punched
the send button.

CHAPTER 8

Oyunga

OYUNGA WAS SITTING in his office at the Sand Resort going through paperwork when the text came in. He looked at it with a self-satisfied grin. He sent her the flowers thinking that the 'How we met' skit he performed with Lily at their engagement party might as well be true somewhere.

I'm not playing any games. I'm just saying the truth.

Her text came back almost immediately.

The truth?

About the magnetic spark.

Mombasa is an extremely hot place. It was nothing more than a heatwave.

Yeah right, a heatwave in an air-conditioned room?

Why do you want to complicate things?

Complicate things? I'm just saying the truth. The truth shall set you free.

I'm not going to do this with you.

What?

In fact I'm erasing this number.

She texted again after a few minutes passed without Oyunga responding.

You won't respond?

I thought you were erasing my number?

The nerve of you men.

Men?

Yeah, you think you can have your cake and eat it too?

There's a cake?

Don't act like you don't know what I mean.

I really don't. Look, I will be in Nairobi this weekend running a few errands, maybe you can explain this cake thing to me over coffee?

I won't be your mistress.

Mistress?

You're an engaged man.

An engaged man can't have a coffee with an acquaintance who felt a heatwave when she saw him?

You felt it too, don't act like I was the only one.

So you agree that our bodies are not receptive to air conditioning? Don't you think that makes us outliers? The more reason to meet.

I will think about it.

She followed up with another text.

No, no, matter-of-fact forget about it. I won't play your games.

Alright, if you change your mind I will be at the Flame Tree Restaurant in Sarova Panafric at exactly 10:00 am on Sunday. If you want to join me for a coffee you're more than welcome.

You're wasting your time and mine.

CHAPTER 9

Prisca

PRISCA HAD MARRIED WELL. Not according to everyone around her but according to herself. She wanted to make it work, not only to prove wrong everyone who told her it couldn't, but for herself. She had roped in a bulking man who filled her head with euphoria and whom she enjoyed in every way.

She loved how he dwarfed other men when they were walking the streets, her hand tied around his arm. She loved the security she felt with him. He might not have been the sharpest tool in the box but he was hers. Everything else was background noise.

Martin was a bit of a bother even for his family. As a kid he was troublesome. More than once, he was suspended from lower primary because of fighting. It got worse in secondary school. He frequently got into verbal altercations with the teachers, and the verbal altercations soon became full-blown fights and that is how he earned his expulsion.

There were other rumors whispered in hushed tones behind closed doors. Martin loved men. It was something his parents thought was a phase, something they thought he would outgrow. But after the third suspension involving a boy he had been caught with in the dormitory bathroom, they started going to bed with the idea.

His dad, having been part of the elite middle class, had taken him under his wing and given him a job in his insurance company but Martin had no brain for business: he spent most of his time flirting with the interns who hadn't a clue who he was. That was okay until it wasn't. He started spending indemnity claims on them and his dad had to get creative yet again.

He started a cyber café for him but soon, all the computers had been sold. At twenty-eight, Martin was only old in age.

His dad got even more creative and opened a hardware but this time he didn't play the fool. He hired a manager and Martin clocked in as a mere employee. Of course there were squabbles but his dad kept him on a very short leash with a meager allowance which he threatened to take away whenever Martin started misbehaving.

It was therefore a welcome sight for Martin's dad when Prisca arrived with her yellow skin, diva-ish demeanor, and law degree, smitten by her newfound love. Prisca's father, on the other hand, had sat her down in their living room with her mother there to support his sentiment.

"I am not sure about this boy you are crazy about."

Her mother adjusted her blue Women's Guild headgear and nodded in agreement.

"We have heard not one report saying that he has been a troubled boy from the very start. Is that what you want to invite into your life?"

Prisca stared at her nails. Her manicure had been freshly done earlier in the day. "I love him and he loves me."

"Prisca, you are a young girl with a promising future. Don't you want someone that deserves you?"

"I want Martin."

"Are you sure that is what you want?"

Prisca shifted in her seat. She was in a bell-shaped green skirt and a purple top. On her feet were lavender platform heels; the same color as her nails. She uncrossed her legs and leaned into her parents.

"Whatever you have heard about him, I can promise it's not true. You know how people can be. And plus, I'm twenty-five, I think I'm grown enough to make my own decisions."

Her father had given her his blessings and let her go knowing that the more you denied a child something, the more they wanted it and the more they painted you as a villain if you stood in their way, even when you knew the thing they wanted was no good.

CHAPTER 10

The Wedding

THE WEDDING WAS lavish and flamboyant. Both families had pulled all the stops to give their children a grand event. Prisca pulled up in a carriage drawn by four horses. She made everybody's head turn in her milk-white ball gown wedding dress whose hem and sleeves were lined with golden lace. Martin had pulled up earlier in a limo escorted by motorbikes. He was in a dark tuxedo that made him look like a bouncer outside a seedy nightclub.

Martin's parents had met every demand Prisca's family had made without much argument. They even met some of the demands with a smile. That should have raised Prisca's eyebrow but it did not. Not when she was living her childhood dream.

Four peacocks spread out their feathers, beautifying the Nairobi Safari Club even further.

The event grounds had been decorated by a seasoned planner. The chairs were arranged so that both sides of the family had their seating areas separate but it still felt intimate. A ring of flowers stood sentry at the apex, with a fountain in the background.

Both sides of the divide had their invite list. The people who were happy for them and the ones they wanted to gloat at. There were a few murmurs on Prisca's side of the family but it was all smiles on Martin's side. You couldn't tell whether they were happy that their son was going to have some stability, or because the whispers that frequently went round about him were being reduced to wind.

The reception took place at Windsor Golf Club. There were croissants and mushroom soup for the starter and for the main course, chicken glazed in honey; goat ribs with a hint of rosemary, garlic, and pepper; sirloin steak; and chapati and *mokimo* for the guests who had come all the way from the village.

It was a feast, but even the feast faded when Martin's dad got up to present the bride and groom with their gifts. A house in the suburbs of Madaraka, fully furnished. He called the couple to the front to present them with the keys and it was not only the house keys but also the keys to a brand new Volkswagen Touareg. Perhaps it was then that Prisca's family knew their daughter's goose was truly cooked but Prisca's face had melted into a crescent-shaped smile.

CHAPTER 11

Honeymoon

THE FIRST TIME they jumped into bed together, Martin thought of his high school sweetheart. The one he was found in the bathroom with. He was on the verge of screaming out his name as he climaxed but Prisca's manicured nails digging into his flesh served as a reminder and stopped him.

They got back from their honeymoon in Egypt and immediately zoomed to the Mara for the wildebeest migration. Martin's dad had increased his allowance almost tenfold and he was now able to do cute things for Prisca. She felt as if she was floating on a cloud.

They only shortened their trip because Prisca had to report to work at Hamilton and Harris Advocates, one of the top law firms in the country. But even then, Martin made sure to wine and dine her every other weekend.

It was a picnic at Karura this weekend, a movie the next, a hotel reservation the weekend after.

She had moved from feeling like a diva to feeling like a princess and now she felt the crown settle gently on her head. She had become a queen.

His family and friends, Marion being one of them, were starting to think they had gotten it all wrong. Marriage, or was it Martin, agreed with her.

It was not long after their wedding when her belly began to swell. It had been a blessing. Prisca did not know it at the time but it was the one thing that would wreck her paradise of a marriage. The one thing that would shatter her crown to pieces.

CHAPTER 12

The Couple

"YOU KNOW WHAT to do when you get to Nairobi, don't you, hon?" Lily said. She was better known by her alias, Quicksilver. Like mercury, she moved liquidly and changed unpredictably.

She circled her fiancé as if she were a vulture and he were carrion while straightening his collar and tying his tie, the scent of her L'Oreal hairspray mixed with her Dior perfume burning his nostrils. That was the difference between her and Marion: Marion was elegant but simple. Lily was in your face with a rambunctious style.

"There are about ten kilos of juice in that briefcase," she said.

Juice was the name they had given to cocaine.

"Make sure it gets to Frankie, he's our distributor in Nairobi. You're taking a private jet from Tom Mboya International Airport to Wilson Airport."

"You won't use the main entrance. You know our contact person there, don't you? He will direct you to a safe entry and our pilot will be waiting for you. Do you want me to run over it again?" she whispered, her breath misting his ear.

"Do you want a bit of something to get you focused?" She stretched her leg out of the flimsy, silk lace cloth that looked like an expensive leso, grabbed Oyunga's hand, and directed it up her inner thighs pushing up one of his fingers inside her and letting out a savage moan. "I won't take long, I promise." Oyunga pushed his finger further up, brushing against brittle pubic hairs and parting her inner lips. Lily let out a rabid groan of approval.

He got up, pushed her against the wall, and undid the knot tying the lace cloth around her waist, yanking it off her forcefully to reveal plump buttocks. Lily arched her back, the dip on the small of her back and the rise of her hips resembling a valley, and her legs split apart out of habit. He plunged in and out of her and as she let out trumpeted moans, he wondered if his aggression was raw desire or if he was trying to prove that he was the man. A man who was in charge, a man who didn't need his fiancée in his ear repeating a brief to him over and over again as if he were a little boy.

CHAPTER 13

Small Argument

SHE STOOD THERE STICKY, the wetness still on her.

"Daddy."

A coarse sound escaped her amid heavy breathing after they were done. She bit her lower lip and watched her fiancé walk to one of the shelves and pick up a pistol. The Browning Hi-Power. He loved its wooden handle and the grip it provided but even more than that, he loved how light and smooth it was.

He removed the cartridge. There were thirteen rounds in the chamber. Oyunga put the pistol back together, wondering how he had gotten into the deep end of all of it. He had a successful career as a chef, yet here he was reassembling a semi-automatic handgun.

"I told you, you don't need a gun. Our friend has provided you with a bodyguard."

They used the name 'friend,' when referring to people in positions of power in government. Governors, senators, judges, army generals. The upper echelon was all in on it.

"How many times will I tell you I don't need a bodyguard?"

"It's for your own safety, hon." Her face had now turned from a face that was dripping with pleasure to one that was full of concern. "Anything can happen out there. We're not selling bread and bananas to a kiosk. This is juice. This is life and death."

"What tells you I don't understand that?" he asked while tucking the Browning Hi-Power into his waistband and covering it with his cobalt blue blazer. "I will be back on Sunday evening. You can wait for me at the airport but I'd prefer it if you didn't. I don't want to trouble you. I'd rather you were here bathing in bath salts, prettying yourself up for me."

"Ten million shillings is not little money, hon. Plus I'm a woman, I can multitask between picking you up at the airport and prettying myself up with bath salts, don't you agree?"

He knew that if she had her way she would be accompanying him to Nairobi. She was the kind of person who wanted to micromanage everything but he had a feeling that she had more pressing business in Mombasa that she didn't want to let on. He picked up the briefcase that had the juice and kissed her on the forehead.

"See you Sunday."

CHAPTER 14

Frankie

THE MOVEMENT AT the airport had gone on without a hitch. Oyunga sat in the private jet, on his phone, talking to Frankie. He had heard tales about him but had never gotten the chance to meet him in person.

Frankie, also known as The Shark, was feared by all the drug barons in Nairobi. It was said he had the strength to split a man's head clear off its neck, the same way a kid disjoints her plastic dolls. Oyunga wanted the meeting to happen immediately after he landed so that he could meet Arigula in the evening and have enough time to clear his conscience before meeting Marion on Sunday morning. "Marion? Will she show?" he murmured to himself.

It was quarter to 3:00 pm when the wheels of the private jet kissed the tarmac at Wilson Airport. The meeting was scheduled for 4:00 pm in an open place in Nairobi.

That was the style of the Shemeji Cartel: everything was done in broad daylight because they believed in the art of hiding in plain sight. After all, if something went wrong they had people in big positions in their pocket. The pilot steered the plane towards a designated area where a grey Land Cruiser was waiting. Oyunga got in and the wheels turned with a screech towards Mombasa road.

"How's the weather in Mombasa? I'm told it's ever hot and the women are ever naked."

"The weather is fine." Oyunga was staring into the cold, dead eyes of The Shark. He was a big, chunky guy who, quite frankly, looked clumsy. His tree-trunk arms and bull-like neck made him look like an amorphous blob of meat.

"You see, Oyunga, that's why a man like me can't live in a place like Mombasa because, quite honestly, I'd fuck my way to death. I have to stay here with Nairobi women. Money, money, money. That's all they cry about. You'd think they're good at making it but no, only spending it."

The Land Cruiser came to a halt next to a busy mall and they both got out.

"You should settle down," Oyunga said as they entered a small café and sat in the gazebo.

"Not every man is cut out to settle down. Can you imagine me in a room with one of these bimbos asking me for money so she can go party? I'd break her neck."

Oyunga wanted to tell him that all the women can't be bimbos but Frankie seemed like the kind of man who thought that his opinion was the law and so Oyunga just laughed it off. He was not here to be a feminist, he was here for business and if the gods were good he would be having a beer with his friend later in the evening and breakfast with Marion the next morning and be back in the arms of his nefarious fiancée same day that evening.

He pushed his briefcase toward Frankie. "Ten kilos of pure juice."

"Ten million cash." Frankie pushed a briefcase towards him. "Could have been more but God gives you only what you ask for."

Oyunga didn't know if Frankie was referring to God or himself.

They shook hands.

"Be careful with that stash, good friend. It's especially risky for a man like you. You know, an unguarded man walking around the streets of Nairobi with that kind of dough."

CHAPTER 15

Oyunga

HE NOW HAD the money in his hands. It was risky either way but he felt money was riskier. Juice and money were both things of great value but few people knew what to do with juice while every Tom, Dick, and Harry knew their way around money.

He clutched the briefcase a little tighter and made a call.

"Did you put it where I asked? … You made sure it was my room, lower drawer, right? … Nobody suspected you, eh? … Alright."

Oyunga ended the call on his secured phone and entered the hotel he was staying in. He said hello to the receptionist, who was also on the Shemeji Cartel's payroll and climbed up the stairs instead of using the elevator. The first thing he did when he entered his room was to reset the safe's password.

He removed the money from the briefcase, put it in his bag then shoved the bag into the upper cupboard and locked it with a simple key. He then removed stacks of counterfeit money from the lower drawer, arranged them in his briefcase, and shoved it into the safe.

It was a trick Lily had taught him. The cartel members were not to be trusted; they were always double-crossing each other. You couldn't trust people like Frankie, people who could fuck their way to death and snap a girl's neck simply because she asked for partying money, now could you?

After, Oyunga went to the pool deck and asked for a neat whisky. He lit his cigarette and sat there puffing rings in the air, wondering how many kids that briefcase he had given to The Shark would ruin. How many would have to steal to afford a hit and how many would be killed because they couldn't pay up? He puffed a thick ring of smoke and felt anxiety engulf him like a dark cloud.

He dug into his pocket and put two of his special pills on his tongue. He washed them down with his whisky and the anxiety left him almost instantly. He crushed the cigarette on the ashtray as a silhouette approached from the distance.

"Mr. Arigula, how are you doing?"

Arigula was in a simple shirt, blue jeans, and sandals. His face looked dehydrated and his aura sagged.

"What are you doing in Nairobi, I thought you're an engaged man?" he chirped, shaking Oyunga's hand and bumping shoulders with him in that way men do.

"Business, my friend, business."

"Business, huh? What is this business? Are you opening a restaurant here or what?"

"Something like that, but what's up with you? How is work?"

"Work is coming along." Arigula did not feel the need to tell his best friend that he had quit his job. He did not want the pity party but even more than that, he was in no mood to feel vulnerable.

"How's your wife, June? I'll tell you right now, you married a firecracker."

"June is okay. You know how women can be sometimes. Hope you have buckled up. How is Lily?"

"Lily is okay. We're pushing through."

Arigula smiled cheekily. "Are you sure you're here for business and not to chase some tail?"

"Come on, boss, you know me better than that." The waitress came around with the menu. Oyunga could sense that Arigula was not in a good place. "The bill is on me today," he said.

They talked for a while in that way men do—just talking on the surface and never really delving into issues because of the fear that it would expose their insecurities. It got late and Arigula excused himself. Oyunga was left staring at an almost empty bar. He thought for a while and decided to go to the hotel's relaxation parlor to get a massage.

"Not deep tissue," he said as he climbed onto the massage table.

He was in no mood for pain. The world, people, and places were full of pain and he did not want to add to that. He wanted something calm and soothing and as the masseur kneaded his body, he escaped into oblivion and found himself moaning the name Marion.

CHAPTER 16

Arigula

JUNE COULD HAVE forgiven his lack of a job if he was not so trifling. She looked at him sitting on the couch and remembered all those days she stayed up waiting for him with a hot meal and he arrived drunk, looking like something the cat dragged in. He would collapse on the sofa and snore, sometimes pissing himself, and she would be the one cleaning after him.

She could have let it slide if it was not for all the times he came home in the wee hours of the night smelling of another woman's perfume. That is what she couldn't understand about men. They were brazen about their affairs and funny enough, they thought it made them more macho. If she ever was trifling, she would be more tactful than that, she thought.

Arigula had had a decent job working for a top hotel in the country. He made sure the curio shops that sold paraphernalia like T-shirts branded, 'I love Kenya' and 'Africa is not a country', and sculpted giraffes, rhinos, and elephants, were well-stocked for the tourists and summer bunnies who frequented the country.

The job was comfortable. It allowed him to travel from county to county looking for new business and sleeping in the best hotels. Honestly, there was not much sleeping because every time he traveled there would be a knock on his hotel room door. Someone in a short skirt, high heels, and a leery smile would be on the other side and Arigula would look at his phone and thank God for Tinder.

An outsider would say he lived a good life. He had an office and decent money that allowed him to drive a Lexus and live in a middle-class neighborhood in Nairobi West. But he felt that life should be deeper than a comfortable job, a house, a car, and a wife. And it was in that way that he woke up one morning, decided that he hated his dull job, and put in his resignation letter.

The first few months were okay. He had some savings stashed away but he quickly burned through them with alcohol and hotel bookings. Now he slept on the couch, not a cent to his name, his wife breathing down his neck and loving every minute of it. He thought of ending it all but then thought it would make his wife too happy and decided to make the best of a bad situation.

CHAPTER 17

Oyunga

OYUNGA HAD A cold shower, wore a grey suit, black shirt, and his Bell and Ross luxury watch. He had breakfast–scrambled eggs and mango juice–then passed by a Quickmart, bought a box of chocolate, took a taxi, and headed towards Flame Tree Restaurant.

He was seated, having a cup of coffee, at exactly a quarter to ten. He busied himself with the newspaper, which was full of election brouhaha. He wondered why elections in Kenya were such a circus. It was never about issues but more like a reality TV show. Aspirants pulling ridiculous manifestos out of thin air. Money flooding the economy. Inflation shooting up. He shook his head because even a kiosk was run better, but then the apple didn't fall far from the tree because here he was, supposedly a 'good citizen', smuggling drugs across counties.

He flipped through the newspaper. There was nothing but acres and acres of jaded journalism, the first sentence of most of the columns suggesting that all the journalist was looking to do was submit an article for the week because it had become routine and after all, food needed to be put on the table.

He shut the newspaper, folded it in two halves, and looked at his timepiece. It was thirty minutes past 10:00 am. *She isn't coming,* he thought and started getting up.

"Hey, what's the hurry?"

Marion approached from behind in a blue denim jacket and a light lime romper that made her eyes sparkle like windows to heaven.

"Well, I was getting up to pull a chair for the fair lady. Aren't you always bickering about how there are no gentlemen left?"

She flashed a smile.

"But seriously, I thought you were not going to show?"

"Well, I had time to kill and I thought why not?"

They hugged and after they sat down he was still dizzy, unsure if it was her Marc Jacobs perfume intoxicating him or her sweet voice which left her lips like a Beethoven symphony. She lifted her neck and their eyes locked, the sexual tension turbulent like a boat in a storm. For a minute, Oyunga forgot about Lily and drug dealing. *I can start my life from zero with her and maybe I can be happy.*

"It's nice to see you. You look dashing," he said.

She lowered her eyelids. "As do you. Lily is doing a good job brushing you up. How is she anyway?"

"Like every engaged girl, electric."

She steadied herself on her seat and struggled out of her denim jacket and in doing so she pushed her chest out in that way girls do and injured Oyunga without realizing it.

"Is it too hot today or is it just me?" she asked.

"If you're feeling hot in Nairobi then you'd have to remove all your clothes in Mombasa."

She chuckled while painting the picture in her head. "You know I never even got to ask what it is you do for a living. You could be a drug dealer for all I know."

"Haha, a drug dealer? Maybe I should try my hand at it. I bet I'd be good at it, maybe even make Pablo Escobar fade in comparison."

She laughed.

"Tell me, Marion, is this what you do? Go around having heatwaves with men? Men you don't even know?"

She eyeballed him again and held his stare as if challenging him into a duel. The face-off felt like electricity coursing through both their veins. "Depends on the man, I guess," she said finally, her mouth curling into a naughty smile.

They talked for a while and when Oyunga looked at his watch, it was heading to 2:00 pm. His flight was scheduled to be airborne in the next hour.

"Is something the matter?"

"My flight leaves in the hour, and oh, before I forget, I got you something."

Oyunga reached for the gift bag beside him and passed it to Marion.

She took a peek. "Thank you. I see you're on a mission to give me cavities."

"You have been living with your sweet self all this time yet here you are without cavities. I think you will be fine."

Marion's mouth curled into a toothy grin as they both got up and hugged. The hug lasted a minute too long.

"We must stay in touch."

"I agree but as friends."
"Of course. Friends, friends."

CHAPTER 18

The Muscle

WHILE OYUNGA WAS having breakfast with Marion, two men were at the reception desk of his hotel. One had a scar on his face. Not the kind of scar you get after you run into a tree or bruise yourself after a fall, no. The kind of scar that suggests brute force. The scarred man was in a black leather jacket, black pants, and black boots and he resembled The Undertaker in every way. He went by the name The Roach.

His accomplice was lean in a gentle kind of way. He was in brown chinos and a simple shirt. He went by the name Zero. He was the brains. Theirs was a case of Lincoln Burrows and Michael Scofield; Brute and Smarts working together for destruction.

"I understand there is a gentleman staying here by the name..." Zero passed a note with the name on it across the desk to the receptionist. It was known that walls had ears.

"I haven't seen such a name in our systems," the receptionist said, playing a little bit of hardball, not knowing that he was only endangering his life by doing so. He knew exactly what was going on—after all he was on the Shemeji payroll—but he was greedy. He thought he might as well get some pocket money from the interaction.

The Roach groaned in a coarse voice.

"You don't understand; we were sent by…" Zero passed another note.

"I don't understand at all."

Zero laughed because he finally caught onto what kind of game he was playing. The receptionist was trifling and he just wanted a bit of under-the-table money.

He gave his partner a look. The Roach put his hand into his jacket and removed fifty thousand bob and passed it to the receptionist.

"Oh, now I remember the name. I have seen the face too. Here is the keycard. I have reset the safe's password. Hope you enjoy your stay and please put in a good word to The Shark for me."

"Will do, will do," Zero said almost in a whisper while leaving the reception desk. He was disgusted by how carelessly the receptionist uttered his boss's name.

They got into Oyunga's room and without wasting time, they opened the safe, got the briefcase out, put the counterfeit money they had brought in their bag in the briefcase, and put what they thought was genuine money in their bag. They locked the safe and left the room, but just before they left the hotel, Zero went back to the reception desk.

"Hey, good old pal. Happy news, our boss just called and he would like to talk to you."

"When?"

"Today, now, actually."

The receptionist's eyes shone with excitement, his face folding into a rugby ball-like grin. He hurriedly got his things and followed them into their tinted black Noah.

The Noah slowed down into a dark alley. The receptionist was the first one to get out. "So, where is he?" he chirped, his voice shaking with nerves and a rivulet of sweat breaking on his forehead. As The Roach got out of the Noah holding a shotgun, the receptionist realized he had gotten into bed with the devil.

The sound that followed was a bullet firing out of the Mossberg 500 shotgun and the next thing, the receptionist was on the asphalt with a pool of blood beside what had been his head.

Zero jumped out of the Noah and rummaged the receptionist's pockets for the 50,000 they had given him.

"You're a talker. Nobody likes a talker."

CHAPTER 19

Lily

WHILE OYUNGA WAS entertaining Marion and Frankie's men were entertaining the receptionist, Lily was dressed up in a raunchy, short, leather skirt and fishnets, rummaging her wardrobe for a whip. She was meeting the head of the cartel, a man who was only referred to as The Scorpion. He loved the name, it inspired fear. It was whispered that he did not have any permanent friends. He always fell out with those close to him because he somehow always ended up stinging them on the back.

Besides being a scorpion and a drug kingpin, he was also a man who had fetishes and Lily was usually the one who satisfied them. She didn't think of it as cheating. On the contrary, she was simply doing her job. Favor from the head of the snake could only mean favor for her and Oyunga.

A long, dark Mercedes S-Class with a Kenyan flag picked her up from their bungalow in the North Coast and within the hour they were pulling up to a manor ranch with government guards saluting as the gates opened and they gained entry.

"He's waiting for you in his study," the butler, or was it the concierge, said as she entered through the door. She had long given up on knowing who was who because The Scorpion kept changing his servants like you would clothes. She closed the door to the study behind her and loosened her long, black robe, underneath it packaged all manner of sins.

"You took your time," a voice behind the chair boomed.

"A lady getting ready is no easy task."

"If you think a lady getting ready is nothing easy, try being Vice President."

"I never said being VP was easy."

"Have you watched the show Game of Thrones?"

He got up from his throne of a leather chair and placed his buttocks on his desk, his hands deep in his pockets. He turned his neck to stare at a painting of the map of the world on the wall.

"Yes, in bits and pieces."

"Being Vice President is a little like being the hand of the king. You do all the drudgery while the king has all the fun."

"You're going to be king soon, you know. Just another five years."

He got up from his desk, walked to the other side of his office, and picked a book from his bookshelf.

"Quicksilver, do you read?" he said while brushing the brittle pages of *The 48 Laws of Power* by Robert Greene.

"What do you mean 'read'?"

Books, people, situations. Do you read?" He did not wait for her to respond. "You should always read. It keeps you sharp and gives you an upper hand over your enemies," he said while returning Robert Greene into the shelf full of books.

"All this is going to be mine," he glanced at the map of the world again, "and when it does you're going to be right here beside me as my queen."

He paused and walked towards Lily. He was a short man whose face gleamed of wealth like a radioactive metal. He was in black pants and a simple shirt whose sleeves he had rolled up to his arms. He almost looked like Lily's little brother. Those were the oddities of this world. The leaders looked nothing like leaders and the led looked like the ones that could lead.

He got close to Lily. She bit her lower lip and dropped her dark robe on the floor.

"You look exceedingly gorgeous," he whispered and she purred.

CHAPTER 20

Oyunga

OYUNGA GOT BACK to his hotel room, got his small key from his pocket, and got the money from the cupboard. He did not bother with the safe; he felt that that would just eat into his time. He went to the reception desk to check out. A lady sat on the other side of the desk.

He got a taxi. It was a style he was quickly adopting; using anonymous taxis instead of cartel-provided cars which he felt were easily traceable. Plus he never could tell what traps they housed.

He made a call to Wilson Airport and was told that the private jet was ready to go and it would be airborne in exactly fifteen minutes, with or without him. "Direct orders from The Scorpion," the voice in the phone cried. It was such things that made him know that he was just another pawn in the circus. He was expendable, a guy who would be six feet under if The Scorpion ordered it.

"Step on the gas, I'll pay you triple."

He got there five minutes to his curfew and sat on one of the leather chairs in the private jet, a glass of whisky in his hand. He was flooded with thoughts. He saw wasted kids in alleys, bodies in graves, and overdosed people with networks of tubes in hospitals. The vividness of the daydream almost made him scream. He went back into his pocket and came out with two of his special pills and washed them down with the whisky as the plane touched down at Tom Mboya International Airport in Mombasa.

CHAPTER 21

Lily

Lily was at the airport waiting. She looked like a popular high school girl in her ponytail-held hair, dark-blue fitting jeans, white Converse shoes, and Mickey Mouse tank-top that stopped shy of her belly button.

She was wearing makeup and extended eyelashes that gave Oyunga the eerie image of her head flying off her neck whenever she blinked.

"How are you, hon?" She kissed him on the lips. "I hope the jet lag is not too bad?"

"It was a short flight. I'm a bit exhausted but that's it."

"That's a big bag," she whispered as the driver opened the door and they got inside their Range Rover. "You think it will be enough for the wedding?"

"More than enough, but aren't we giving seventy percent of it to The Scorpion?"

"I spoke to him and let's just say we can keep fifty percent."

"Fifty percent? How do you go off getting favors from this shadow of a man? Or is there something you're not telling me?"

"Come on, hon, this is no time to be jealous. The Scorpion is a generous man, he knows our wedding is on the horizon." Her tongue glossed her cherry-red lips. "Plus you know my tongue is very smooth."

"Well, let's hope he stays generous and your tongue gets smoother than an eggshell because I could really use its smoothness tonight."

She laughed.

"You bet, and about the wedding, I'm thinking we do it next month."

"Isn't that too soon?"

"Don't you want to make it official as soon as possible?"

"Aren't we living together, aren't you already behaving like a wife and I like a husband? We're practically married, aren't we?" he said as they got out of the car and entered their bungalow.

"I want it solemnized. I want that certificate and that white gown and envy from all my friends. I'm a typical girl, Oyunga."

"Okay, okay, but just know I'm going back to Nairobi next week." He paused, thinking of a quick lie. "I bumped into my friend and there's this restaurant that I think might be worth our while."

"A restaurant? Don't we have enough money and shouldn't you be worrying about our wedding instead?"

"What do you mean, 'A restaurant' and 'Don't we have enough money'? This is a good deal. One of those once-in-a-lifetime opportunities and I feel it will slip away if we don't move quickly."

"And you can't close it here, or have one of our people do it for you?"

"Come on, hon, you know I'm a hands-on person," he said, moving close to her, reducing her tone to a whisper, and grabbing her backside. "I have to look at the place, see what we can do with it, and get the paperwork going."

"How about I accompany you?"

"Hon, don't you trust me? Do you want word to go round that I'm whipped?" he asked then kissed her lips softly.

"And how long will this trip of yours be?" she mumbled while unzipping his pants.

"I'll go on Wednesday, work on the deal on Thursday and Friday and come back on Saturday."

"That's a long time."

"Well, good things take time, hon."

She was not stupid. She could tell something was up, something other than her fiancé's manhood.

CHAPTER 22

Prisca

PRISCA'S STOMACH WAS now bigger than her buttocks. The fun and sex took a hiatus and Martin started coming home at absurd hours, three or four nights a week. He disappeared from his hardware job altogether. The manager did not raise alarm about it. He found it was easier to manage things without him around.

Before going home, he would sometimes pass by a pub and have one for the road. It cleared his mind and made him feel like an ordinary citizen.

The first time he came home late he found Prisca asleep. The second time, she just groaned and asked where he had been before going back to sleep. But the third time she was ready for him.

Martin was not even tipsy. He had had two bottles of Tusker and gotten into their Volkswagen Touareg. He drove along Uhuru Highway towards Madaraka thinking how lucky a man he was. Here he was, having been troubled since childhood, but the stars seemed to be aligning for him. He had a beautiful, educated wife expecting his child, a house in a good neighborhood, and a car he did not lift a finger to own, and… He smiled, imagining the look on his dad's face if he knew that he was more than just a fuck-up son.

He hooted and the watchman opened the gate. He got to the door and as usual, fumbled with his keys before opening the door. It was pitch-black inside. He groped for the switch but before he could locate it, the lights came on. His beloved wife was seated on the sofa in a flimsy negligee. Her head and upper body hidden behind her mountain of a pregnancy.

"Is this any time to come home to your pregnant wife?" she barked.

The clock on the wall read five minutes to three am.

"I'm sorry, sweetheart. I passed by the pub to blow off some steam," he said calmly.

"Some steam, eh? Is that the name you've given to the prostitute you fuck?"

He went silent, his anger rising.

"I can smell her perfume all the way here. Is that why you have not been touching me?"

His face went blank. He wasn't guilty of bedding a prostitute but he was guilty of other, more heinous things and Prisca could smell it on him.

"Get out. Go back to your prostitute."

"This is my house. I am going to bed."

"Your house? Huh, besides being a cheat you're also a comic. Is that the same way you brag to that prostitute with your father's car and job?"

He did not know how it happened but one moment he was going to the bedroom to sleep and the next he was slapping her silly across the face. He did not remember if he used his fist. It was all hazy now as the watchman rushed into the house after Prisca's screams hit fever-pitch.

CHAPTER 23

Marion

MARION SAT BEHIND her desk with one hand supporting her chin and the other tinkering with a biro. She was just from a meeting with a client who was dissatisfied with everything. She was dissatisfied with the artwork concepts, the TVC ads, and the radio voice-overs. If you asked Marion she would have told you that the client was also dissatisfied with the sunshine and the clouds the day had to offer.

Ad agencies and client relationships were a lot like human relationships: when the relationship wasn't working the party that wanted out brought all manner of excuses to the table. She was of the opinion that if a client wanted to leave there was nothing you could really do but let them go. You could call Rembrandt to do their artwork and they would still frown.

She swiveled in her chair, wondering whether she should do an email to Sandeep and tell him the client would leave sooner or later and that it was better for them to cut their losses now before they were left with egg on their faces.

Marion felt that she had made sure her client got the very best from their agency. She had a feeling that after the client left they would realize that the grass wasn't always greener on the other side and they would soon be back.

She steadied her chair and started putting her points down when her phone buzzed.

Guess who is in town?

You just left for Mombasa last week?

Well, I can't seem to be able to stay away from a certain someone.

Your wife?

I don't have a wife.

You're engaged?

She's called a fiancée.

Isn't that the same thing?

How's dinner this evening?

She thought for a moment and decided that she could use a break to unwind from the pressure of dealing with clients who didn't know what they wanted. Clients who thought ad agencies were charity organizations and clients who thought they knew everything even though they had outsourced a third party to work on their behalf.

She thought for a minute and realized she also needed to put Oyunga on the straight and narrow path. Whatever it was he thought was going to happen between them wasn't going to happen while he was still engaged to be married to another woman.

Pick you at your office at 6:30?

That's a bit early for me.

Alright, meet me at Om Café, Dada Street, 8 pm? That works.

CHAPTER 24

Lily

WHILE OYUNGA WAS texting Marion, Lily was on the phone with The Shark. She knew Frankie was volatile but she also understood that sometimes it was necessary to work with your enemies to accomplish a goal.

"Quicksilver, long time no see. I heard you got engaged. Are you still as beautiful as I remember you?"

Lily and Frankie had a bit of history. They had done assignments together and let's just say during assignment breaks, things had happened.

Lily never really enjoyed Frankie though; he was not sensual. He made love to a woman the same way he handled an AK-47.

"I need a favor from you, Frankie."

"Favor from me? You know I don't just give out those to anybody, Sweet Cheeks, but for you, I'm willing to bend the rules."

"Oyunga is in Nairobi."

"Don't mention that name to me, Quicksilver. You know the very thought of you with someone else makes my skin crawl."

Besides being angry about Lily's relationship, Frankie was also nursing injuries after being outfoxed by Oyunga.

"Come on, you're a big boy, don't tell me you're jealous. Plus that was a long time ago."

"A long time ago but it still burns in my mind like it was a minute ago."

Lily might have hated her encounter with Frankie, but Frankie had loved every second of it. She was the first woman to put up a fight. The first woman to resist his dominance and he found that magnetic.

"Let's get down to business, Frankie. Are you going to help me or not?"

"Go on, Sweet Cheeks, shoot."

"Oyunga is in town, I need him tailed. I need a report on everywhere he goes and with whom. I need a report on everything he does while there. If he sneezes, I want it in the damn report."

"You don't trust your loverboy there, Sweet Cheeks? Mistrust is not the best foundation for a marriage, wouldn't you agree?" he said with a laugh.

"Just do the damn job, Frankie."

"Hey, hey, watch your tone. What's in it for me?"

"Name your price."

"I don't want money, I have enough of that."

"Then what do you want?"

"A night with you."

Lily thought for a moment. It never stopped baffling her how most men could do almost anything when sex was on the table. She smiled because she could keep sex as just sex. She was also not opposed to using her body if it got her what she wanted. People used their skills to get things, their contacts and networks to go places, why not bodies?

"Consider it done."

CHAPTER 25

Oyunga

OYUNGA SAT AT Om Café with Marion. He was in an ash grey shirt, black khakis, brown loafers, and had a beige scarf around his neck. He looked like a model out of a page in GQ magazine. Marion looked like a sexy teacher in her yellow crop top, neon A-line skirt, and mustard rubber shoes.

"Come on, Marion, you can't be serious," Oyunga egged on.

Marion was saying that she had never eaten arosto with bananas on one big plate like they were doing now.

"You must be very spoilt, Mari."

"No, no, no, I'm the only child and nothing was handed to me. I have had to work for everything I have but men think otherwise. When they see you up there on top of the corporate ladder they think you must have slept with a thousand men." She paused and stared at Oyunga, getting lost in him as he got lost in her.

"We have to get serious, Oyunga."

"I'm all for getting serious."

She laughed. "Not in that way. What we're doing is wrong."

"What?"

"Whatever we're doing here. This has to stop."

"We're in too deep, Mari, we might as well swim."

"We're not in too deep."

He held her hand. "What is it going to take?"

"You're engaged."

"I can get out of an engagement."

"I don't know, Oyunga. Men say one thing and do the other. You know you can't have your cake and eat it too and I wouldn't be comfortable being with someone who is set to be married. It's like you're going through a crisis and I'm the petrol propelling your speed boat.

"Alright, I will think about it. Let's change the subject."

"How is work?"

He wondered if he should tell her that he sold ten kilos of pure cocaine the other day and got ten million Kenya shillings in exchange. He wondered if he should tell her that he was a drug dealer and he moonlighted as a chef just to keep up appearances. He wondered if he should tell her that the cartel he worked for was responsible for ninety percent of the drugs in Kenya and sometimes it ate him up to the point of suicide but then he had these special pills that kept him sane.

"Work is great. I'm working on a new menu and crossing my fingers that it picks up."

"How come I have never tasted your culinary delicacies, Mr. Great Chef?"

"My delicacies?" He leaned forward, his muscles bulging

out of his ash grey shirt. "You could taste my delicacies if, I don't know, you invited me to your place and allowed me to take over your kitchen."

"I could invite you to my place but I know you will start other things that shouldn't be on the menu for an engaged man."

"I promise to behave."

Oyunga settled the bill and they got up and started walking towards the door. In the corner of the restaurant, Zero was pretending to take selfies but on close inspection was taking pictures of them. Outside, The Roach took their photos as they entered Marion's Toyota Harrier. The illicit duo got into a Jeep and tailed them as they drove towards Kilimani.

CHAPTER 26

Cooking Session

THEY SAT ON the couch to eat the buttered chicken that Oyunga had prepared.

"This is really good," Marion tee-heed amidst mmmh's and ahh's.

For a minute, Oyunga had thought he might have forgotten how to cook. At the Sand Resort, his work had been reduced to managerial tasks while in their house in Mombasa they had a cook even though they rarely ate there. They were always being invited to events and people's houses–people who needed favors, people who wanted to get their foot in the business.

"I'm glad you're enjoying it," he said. He put his plate down and moved closer to her but Marion swatted him away like you would a mosquito.

"No, Oyunga, we said this was not happening."

She got up and moved to another couch and picked up the TV remote.

"What do you want to watch?"

"I want to watch you."

"Come on, be serious."

"What do you have?"

"Well, we could watch Grey's Anatomy."

"Jesus Christ, Mari, I'd rather talk about the books on your bookshelf." He got up. "Do you read a lot?"

"I do. I always have a book in my bag."

He picked up a book on the shelf. "Hmm… *The Fault in Our Stars* by John Green." He put it back and pulled out another one. "*Milk and Honey* by Rupi Kaur. You don't read African literature, do you?"

"I do, but I feel as if the community of African writers is too sensitive. They're always wrangling about being excluded by Europe yet clamoring for that European prize, what is it called again, ah, yes, The Caine Prize for African Writing. I mean, just write spectacularly and people will read your work regardless. Besides, art is universal. The cultures might be different but humanity isn't."

"Nice speech there. So who is your favorite author?"

"Currently, or of all time?"

"Of all time."

I would have a hard time picking between Mario Puzo, F. Scott Fitzgerald, and Donna Tartt, yourself?"

"Anthony Bourdain, but I guess that has a bias on food." He put Rupi Kaur back after brushing through the pages and walked towards his seat.

"You want to say you don't have anything else we can watch, not even an animation?"

"I think I have a Trevor Noah stand-up."

"Okay, put him on."

It was late when the stand-up ended. Marion got up and led Oyunga to the guest bedroom.

"See you in the morning. One more thing, how do you like your eggs, sunny-side up or scrambled?"

"Scrambled, and thank you for everything, Mari, I mean it. I had a great time."

"Me too, Oyunga. Me too."

Marion went to bed but she couldn't sleep. She had put on a good act of swatting Oyunga away but she was burning to be touched, to be caressed, and to be ravished. It had been quite a while. For the most part, all her energy was immersed in her work but having a man in the house reminded her that she was a sexual being just like any other person.

Indecent thoughts flooded her. She writhed and tossed and turned, her body crying out for Oyunga the same way lungs cry out for oxygen. She thought about going to the guest bedroom but stopped herself, the thought of how desperate she would look jumping at her.

On the other side of the wall, Oyunga was snoring. No for him meant no. If he were like other men who thought 'No' meant 'Yes' and 'Yes' meant 'Yes', he wouldn't be snoring; he would be lighting up the sheets with the love of his life.

CHAPTER 27

Scrambled Eggs

Marion Walked Into the guest bedroom carrying scrambled eggs and juice on a platter as Oyunga had requested. She was in a silver negligee that revealed traces of her nipples. She walked barefoot into the room. The radio was on, music was filtering in through the speakers in low volume and Rihanna and Drake's *Work* was playing: '…If you had a twin I would still choose you. I don't wanna rush into it, if it's too soon. But I know you need to get done, done, done, done if you come over…' Her heart did a jig. She felt as if Oyunga was whispering those very words directly into her ear.

"Oyunga? Oyunga, where are you?" she called.

"I'm in the bathroom."

The heaviness of his Luo accent brought her to life, made her nipples stand erect and her female delicates throb like a second heartbeat.

She had been restless all night and she felt the mere sight of Oyunga would make her knickers combust into an inferno, only she wasn't wearing any.

"What are you doing in the bathroom?"

"Having a shower or picking apples. I can't decide which one it is."

"Are you almost done?"

"No, I just started a few seconds ago."

Her skin felt hot and sticky. Her breathing grew erratic. She placed the plate of scrambled eggs and juice on the dresser. She slipped out of her negligee, revealing an ocean of dark chocolate skin, smooth as velvet, tremendous breasts, and a lusty figure. She pushed open the bathroom door and Oyunga's mouth fell to the floor and his manhood almost hit the ceiling.

CHAPTER 28

Oyunga

ON THE FLIGHT back to Mombasa, Oyunga was in a state of nirvana. He could still feel Marion's hands caressing his head, going down to the nape of his neck and squeezing his muscles. He could still feel her kissing his lips and sinking to her knees to take his manhood in her mouth, almost making him detonate like a nuclear warhead.

He was a man who could last long, at least with Lily, but with Marion it was a different kettle of fish. He found himself spilling his seed after the fourth thrust and only lasted a bit longer on the second and third rounds.

We should have used protection, he thought. He then thought he could trust Marion, he also thought he could trust his fiancée. *His fiancée?* He started thinking of a fib that he would feed Lily and then dozed off.

CHAPTER 29

Arigula

IF YOU HAD told Arigula that he would have grown up to be a photographer, he would have looked at you and laughed. Not because he didn't think much of photography but because to him it was a hobby, something you did to pass time, not to make a living.

During his work travels, when he was not too busy working or entertaining a tryst, he would whip out his phone and take pictures of the landscape, wild animals, and the revelers at the hotel he stayed in. He would then put his phone back in his pocket and mind his own business—business that often had long legs, delicate curves, and full lips.

Sometimes a few of those women stumbled upon the photos and told him they were spectacular, but then he felt they said it in a way that anybody in their position would. Anybody who was sleeping in a five-star hotel on someone else's tab, that is. So he never paid it any mind.

Until one of them convinced him to open an Instagram account.

Out of a job and a hundred posts in, there was a heartbeat but nothing solid. June loved to berate him. "How is that Instagram career of yours coming along? Wash the dishes and clean the house. I will give you your money's worth, promise," she would say while picking up the key to her Mazda Demio. Beside her car was Arigula's Lexus collecting dust because income from washing dishes and cleaning the house, it turned out, could not fuel a car.

He had thought marriage would be something different. He had expected a friend and a cheerleader but instead, it had become a competition and now he needed to win more than ever. That's how he found himself on a car-selling website putting his Lexus up for sale. In a week it had a buyer.

The following week he bought a digital single-lens reflex camera, an Apple MacBook Pro, lenses and lighting modifiers, and he was in business. He felt if nothing else, the gear would help improve his craft.

"What a waste of good money," June had murmured.

CHAPTER 30

The Couple

LILY WAS WAITING for her husband in the house with a smile.

"How was the trip, hon?"

"Ah, the trip was fine."

"Did you close the restaurant deal?"

"You know how these things are. It's a process. It will take more time than I thought."

"Oh, that's a shame. Come and sit. The cook made something for us. I know you're exhausted and hungry."

His fiancée had her spasms of pleasantness but he felt that she was going overboard with it today. He decided to play along and squeeze everything he could from it because such moments were fleeting.

They sat and ate pork with pilau. Afterward, she opened a bottle of Merlot and led him to the bedroom.

She had missed him after all and there was no need for Marion to come in between them. She had urges and she needed them satisfied.

"How was it?" she asked after he finished pumping and was breathing heavily beside her.

"Good, I guess."

"Good, you guess? Better than that heifer, Marion, I'm sure?"

His mouth flew open. This was his get-out-free card but he was like every other man.

"I know how it looks, but it's not what you think."

"Don't apologize."

"I can explain."

"No need. Our people are headed to Kilimani to take care of that problem. Let that be the last time you make a fool of me."

"Take care of the problem?"

"You didn't think I would just sit and let some parasite come in between us, did you, hon?"

"But she's your best friend's friend."

"Who slept with my husband. You think I care about some friendship after that?" Lily asked and Oyunga could taste the spite in her mouth. He shot out of bed, picked his phone, and ran to the balcony. He locked the door behind him and dialed Marion.

CHAPTER 31

Marion

"Marion, you have to get out of there quickly," Oyunga's voice boomed.

"Hi, Oyunga, you just woke me. How was your flight?"

"Marion. Listen. You have to get the hell out of there as quickly as you can."

"What's going on?"

"You won't understand; I'll explain everything later," he said, short of breath.

"I'm not going anywhere till you tell me what the hell is going on."

"I'm a drug dealer, Marion, a drug dealer. My fiancée has discovered what we were up to over the weekend and she has sent hitmen to eliminate you."

"What?"

"You need to get to safety as quickly as possible. Listen, forget about your car, it might be wired with explosives. I'm sending my contact; he should be there in less than ten minutes. He will be in a red sedan…"

"What is happening, Oyunga? A drug dealer? Hitmen? Explosives? How long do I have?" she said, panicked.

"Listen, Mari, don't panic. You have to stay calm and think clearly. You have very little time; you have to move. They could be there even as we speak."

Marion felt as if she was having a nightmare. She got up, quickly wore a denim jacket over her negligee, and slipped into flat shoes. She picked her handbag and limped outside after knocking her knee against the coffee table.

It was raining torrents. Thunderstorms were booming and stripes of lightning flashing. She was going to die, she thought, if not from the hitmen, then from electrocution by lightning. She was running now, soaking wet, and trying to avoid the road that was completely lit up by street lights. As she ran, a car in the distance flashed its headlamps and came to a stop next to her. She let out a rabid scream full of fear.

CHAPTER 32

The Ghost

It was the red sedan Oyunga had told her about. She got in and the car turned around, drifting on the slippery road.

"Don't worry, I have been sent by Oyunga," a voice on the driver's seat, scratchy and rough, droned.

She couldn't make out the driver. His hat was tipped to the front so that it masked half his face.

"Thank you," she said amid short breaths.

They hadn't driven a hundred yards when they passed a dark Noah. The Noah slowed down, made a U-turn, and started chasing them.

Marion realized they were being chased after the black Noah hit the red sedan on the bumper, making the car hurtle off the road and throwing her from one side of her seat to the other, almost knocking her out of the window.

She let out a bloodcurdling scream.

"Wear your seatbelt, ma'am," the driver said casually as if they were having mango juice in Nairobi's traffic.

The car was now skidding from side to side on Argwings Kodhek Road and Marion kept doing the rosary. She let out another scream after the Noah hit them again, this time from the side. The red sedan sped off the road, almost hitting a street pole and plunging into a ditch, but the driver managed to steer it back onto the road.

"I'm getting tired of this," the driver muttered.

Marion had a deer-in-the-headlights look. She was now frozen stiff, resembling an inanimate thing. They were now speeding on the stiff slope that is Valley Road and she felt as if the wheels were coming off. The driver accelerated and swerved as the Noah came at them in full tilt, ready to smash them to a stop.

He swerved the car again, pulled the handbrake and the sedan came to an abrupt stop and did a ninety-degree turn. He put the handbrake down and stepped on the gas towards Ralph Bunche Road while the Noah flew in full tilt along Valley Road.

"Madam, are you okay?"

"Have we lost them?" Marion asked, her body skittish with nerves.

"They won't be bothering us for a while," the driver said. He came to a halt in front of a ramshackle building, half made of bricks and half made of iron sheets. "You'll spend the night here, it's safe. I'm going to make arrangements for your flight to Eldoret. I will be back early tomorrow morning, say 5:00 am, to pick you up. Try and have some rest, ma'am."

CHAPTER 33

The Couple

"Is this what we're doing? You're willing to compromise our relationship for that heifer?"

"She doesn't deserve to die for my mistakes. Break up with me and leave her out of it."

"There are no breaks in this relationship. You're in this till the end."

"I'm not in anything," Oyunga said while packing his clothes into a bag. "I'm a chef, remember? Not a drug dealer. I can get out anytime I want."

"And who do you suppose will supply you with your special, little pills, huh?" she said. "What do you think The Scorpion will do when he hears you opted out? Smile and send you a fruit basket?"

"He can do whatever he wants."

"A bullet in between your eyes. That's what you'll get."

"I'll take my chances."

"What about our wedding, Oyunga?"

"Wedding? Get married to a sociopath? I think not."

"You're the one who cheated on me."

"Then break up with me," he said while turning the doorknob.

Lily thought of chasing him but decided against it.

"He will be back," she murmured to herself.

CHAPTER 34

Lovebirds

I COULD HAVE DIED, Oyunga, I could have died!" Marion was frantic on the phone.

"I had a boulder in my chest at the thought of something happening to you."

"Oyunga."

"Are you okay?"

"They could have killed us."

"The person who picked you up is a good friend of mine, he's arranging your flight to Eldoret."

"They could have killed us, Oyunga, and for what? For what?"

"Listen to me carefully, Mari. They will probably go back to your house and ransack it. You can't go back or do any kind of transaction. You have to stay put."

"Why are you doing this to me, Oyunga? I was perfectly happy without you."

"Listen to my contact person and don't give him a hard time because the more time we waste the easier we make it for them to find us."

"Mmmh-hmmm," she screeched, deluged by everything that was happening.

"Keep warm, Mari. I'm taking a flight from Mombasa to Eldoret. I will meet you there and we will figure this out."

Oyunga had to move fast. It wouldn't be long before they contacted all the airports. As far as Lily was concerned, he was just cooling off, taking a break the way you do when a job becomes overwhelming. But as far as he was concerned, he was done with all of it. The drugs, the pretense, ruining people's lives. He was done.

As he headed towards the airport he thought for a moment that he could open a small restaurant and live in peace, somewhere like Kisumu. The cartel's virus had not yet spread there. He and Marion could have a real chance to start over.

CHAPTER 35

Arigula

WHEN HE GOT his first paying assignment you would have expected him to call his wife with pomp and excitement. He did call June but it was to ask for a divorce. Nobody was emotional about it; neither party cried or spent long nights wondering why. It was mechanical, almost the way a car stops working and nobody goes on a tangent because everyone knows it stopped working because the engine was faulty.

Arigula had moved into a servant's quarters in Hurlingham, an upper-middle-class settlement where you woke up in the morning and found people walking their dogs or having a morning jog.

He had decided that he would live an artistic life. His living room did not have a television screen but a big painting of a nude woman. He had bought it from a budding artist for twenty thousand bob and every time he looked at it, it looked different.

It was a big point of conversation whenever he brought a woman over. He was starting to forget the spiel he was feeding them.

"It is from the highlands of Croatia. It was painted with a feather."

"Oh, that? That is the impression of how fleeting life can be."

On the other side of the wall was a bookstand. He wasn't much of a reader but he now found himself collecting photography books and camera souvenirs and they all went on that shelf.

He had never felt more alive than he was feeling at that moment. He went to the shelf again and looked at a Charles Dickens' novel titled *Great Expectations*. He had gotten it from one of his many girlfriends. He traced his forefinger along the spine of the book. Society's expectations were all wrong. He had thought he would be happy with a decent job, a wife, a house, and a car, but he had been miserable. Now here he was, in nirvana with just a camera and a nude painting to his name.

CHAPTER 36

Lovebirds

"Why did you do this to me?"

Marion was punching Oyunga on the chest in small sporadic movements.

"I was perfectly fine, Oyunga, perfectly fine."

"I'm sorry, Mari. I didn't know my fiancée was cuckoo."

"What now, Oyunga? What now?"

"For now I can't be Oyunga and you can't be Marion." He handed her an ID and a passport, new and crisp, as if they were freshly minted from the factory. He had gotten them made a long time ago in case things got dicey and he and Lily needed to disappear. Marion was now Zawadi and he was Bakari.

"The photos are not clear so I think you can get away with impersonating Lily for now. Come, we need to buy a second-hand car, something with grit and that does not attract attention."

Marion was pulling her hair out. She felt as if she was in a horror film she hadn't auditioned for.

"Oyunga, I thought you were a chef. Why should I even believe that this is for my own good and not another one of your cartel's twisted schemes?"

"The name is Bakari, thank you very much." Oyunga grinned but Marion had no time for his japes.

"I can't believe you're making fun. This is my life you're playing with. Why?"

"Look, Mari, drugs are everywhere in Kenya under the Shemeji Cartel banner. The cartel goes all the way up to government officials and it's headed by someone only known as The Scorpion. I'm just a pawn in all this. How would I benefit from saving you only to give you up?"

"And your contact person?"

"A good friend of mine. He'll make it look like we've disappeared from the face of the earth until things cool off."

They walked to a car yard and bought a Nissan Datsun under their new monikers.

"I hope you're ready for a road trip, Zawadi?"

"Where to?"

"Kisumu. A remote place called Ndukiya. Do you like fish, Zawadi? I hope so because that is all we will be eating for some time now."

"And what will we do in Ndukiya, Oyunga, start a kebab cafe that doubles as a drug depot?"

"I wouldn't mind some tilapia kebab for starters. I'm starving."

She shrugged. "I just want a shower and some rest, since the truth, it seems, is hard to come by."

"I have told you everything I know."

"And this money we're using?"

"Remember the time I came to Nairobi? This is the money I got from the deal I made."

"Drug money?"

"It sounds bad when you put it like that. Think of it as survival money, money that will make sure we stay alive while we figure things out and get some good tilapia kebab while at it."

"God help us," Marion said while doing the rosary.

CHAPTER 37

Cutting Ties

"What happens when my relatives or my colleagues try to reach me?" Marion howled. The car shook and heaved as they left the tarmac and turned into another road that didn't seem fit for pedestrians, leave alone motorists.

"Parents?"

"I was brought up by a single mom. She passed a while back but I have an uncle."

"You're a clever woman, Mari, I'm sure you can come up with a story for your colleagues. And uncles, I figure, are never that invested in anything to do with relatives that involve effort."

"What about you?"

"Haha. Look who is pretending to be concerned about my affairs?"

"What happens when your family calls you, or is it part of the cartel?"

"Family?"

"Yeah."

"I'd appreciate it if we didn't talk about my family."

"So that's how it works, huh?" Her hands were crossed under her breasts and she had a scornful look on her face. "I break down my entire family tree for you and you say nothing about yours?"

Oyunga was staring dead ahead. The car's windshield hit a low hanging branch.

"It's just something I prefer not to talk about. Maybe someday I will tell you about it."

There was a silence before Marion spoke again.

"What about my friends?"

"Prisca?"

"Yes, Prisca."

"She always came around to visit before her marriage but I rarely see her nowadays, how is she?"

"Happy in her marriage."

He relaxed his muscles. One hand was on the wheel and the other on the gear. He looked at Marion, still in her negligee which was tucked up her thighs, revealing her bruised knee.

"Are you okay?"

She looked at him with her lips pursed and furrowed her brow.

"What did you think about the guy she married? There was a lot of noise that he was no good and honestly I still have my fingers crossed."

"Does he make her happy?" Oyunga asked.

"She seems happy. Maybe we got him wrong. I just hope that ship of happiness never hits an iceberg."

"That's the problem with society."

"What?"

"We sing to people to get married then after they do we put a timer on the relationship. We're a poisonous society."

"I'm just looking out for my friend."

"I know."

"You should leave this drug business and become a motivational speaker, you have the knack for it."

Oyunga laughed.

"I loved my job, you know. I used to lead a team. I used to get mail and people used to call me madam."

"I like how you talk about it in the past tense. That says you're committed to this and you love being alive a little more than I thought."

CHAPTER 38

Prisca

H_ER LIP WAS BUSTED_, raw, and pink. Her left eye was black and bulging. Her face looked like rising dough. Prisca was the kind of woman who liked to seem prim and proper even when things were going haywire and even as she sat there, in the same room where her dad had told her Martin was no good, she still tried to conceal things.

She sat on one side of the room with her parents. Martin and his parents sat on the other.

Martin's parents looked apologetic and embarrassed, as if they were the ones who had committed the assault. Martin's face was staring at the floor, burning with rage. He did not dare lift it for his in-laws to see.

"Where do you get the nerve to hit a pregnant woman?" Prisca's dad roared.

Martin's face remained on the floor.

"I think our daughter should stay with us until this is re-solved," Prisca's mother added.

"You know how it can be with a young marriage. I'm sure we can resolve this," Martin's dad spoke. His mind rushed to his son's old days and he dreaded it. "Son, speak up. What happened?"

"She provoked me," Martin mumbled, his face still stuck on the floor.

"You are provoking me now, should I punch your teeth in?" Prisca's dad shot.

"What was it about?" Martin's mom was looking directly at Prisca, willing her to speak to her woman to woman.

"He, he, came home late. He has been doing it often. I think he's seeing another woman," Prisca stammered.

"Son, are you seeing another woman?" his dad asked with a gentle hand on his son's arm knowing all too well that couldn't be the case.

"No, just one or two late-night drinks to blow off some work steam. Nothing else."

Martin's dad did not feel it was necessary to discuss that his son was rarely seen at the hardware nowadays.

"I don't think we will resolve anything today. Like her mom said, our daughter is going to stay with us until she decides otherwise. If she decides she will come back to you, I don't want to hear that you lifted your hand against her. If I do, I will have to lift mine as well. And if she decides she doesn't want to come back to you, well, there is nothing I can do but honor her wish."

Prisca disappeared to one of the rooms in their house. Martin's parents whispered something in his ear and he got up and went outside. The parents were left whispering to each other. Martin's parents talked for the most part. They felt today's children needed a lot of guidance.

Prisca's dad did not speak much; his anger could not allow him to. He hoped his daughter would come to her senses and stay with them. He prayed this would be the last time he saw this lot of swine.

Prisca was back with her husband the following week.

CHAPTER 39

Lovebirds

FOUR MONTHS CAME and went. They had gotten a small piece of land in Ndukiya and built a shack. There was a small stream behind their house and a few miles up the stream was Lake Victoria. Marion was doing a decoupage of a flower on a pot she was molding using the clay from the stream.

"That's an incredibly decent pot," Oyunga said from his wicker chair. He was going through a newspaper that was a week old.

"Thank you. It's called art and craft."

"Haha, is it something you've always done?"

"I like to create and mold things. It calms my soul and quiets my mind."

"Would you have preferred to be in the arts sculpting as opposed to advertising?"

She laughed.

"Well, right now I'm living with a drug kingpin so I don't know what I would prefer."

"I'm serious."

"Advertising is also an art, Oyunga. Creative concepts, branding, strategy: they all require imagination. Of course most days are routine but other days feel like a blank canvas begging you to leave your footprints."

She got up slowly, poured water from a mtungi and washed her hands in a basin. She then reached for a piece of cloth and proceeded to dry them.

Oyunga put his newspaper aside and leaned forward. "I know this wasn't what you asked for, Mari. I know it hasn't been easy living with me; groping in the dark, not knowing where this will lead you. Telling your uncle you flew out, resigning. I know it has been hard."

She smiled and held Oyunga's hand. A lot of things had been going through her head when they first came to Nduki-ya. She was here with a drug dealer whom she knew very little about besides what he was telling her, and she had almost gone berserk. But her heart softened as the days wore on. Oyunga handled her gently, like a blooming flower, and that peeled back her layers and revealed an enchanting vibrancy she didn't know existed.

"Oyunga, don't worry too much about the past. Thank God for this moment, for the blessing he has given us amidst all the chaos," she said, now rubbing her tremendous stomach.

"Did you finally find out the gender or are you still headstrong about leaving it a mystery?"

"I couldn't help it. I confirmed it this morning during my routine checkup."

Oyunga was still awed that even with her tremendous

stomach, she could still take the Nissan Datsun and drive to Kisumu city for checkups. Oh, how she protested when he volunteered to take her.

"Is that why you're glowing like this?"

"Twins, Oyunga, we're having twins. A boy and a girl."

Oyunga got up from his seat, grinning. He crashed to the floor on one bended knee and rubbed Marion's stomach. "You're both going to be as clever as your mom and as charming as your daddy."

"We should tell somebody. If not my uncle, your family."

"My family?"

"Yes, your family."

Oyunga got up. "I'm an orphan, Mari. My parents deserted me when I was little." He sat back down on his wicker chair, bowed his head, and hunched his shoulders. "I was on the streets till a Good Samaritan came by and took me to a children's home. He is the only family I know."

"Is he the contact person?"

"Yes."

"I'm sorry."

"My mother, or whatever you would call her, gave me a call a few months ago and I dismissed her. Can you believe the nerve of that woman, a call after all these years? Where was she when I was going hungry, getting rained on, wearing sacks for clothes, people treating me like scum? Where was she?"

"She is still your mother, Oyunga. You should at least give her a listening ear."

"No, Marion, she's a stranger. Dead to me, do you hear me? Dead."

Marion resolved to put the issue on pause for the moment. She would crawl back little by little until Oyunga caved in. She was the result of a single mom and she cherished the love of a mother. She knew what it meant and she wanted the man she loved to know how that kind of love felt as well.

"Enough of that," Oyunga barked. "We should celebrate this gift that God has blessed us with."

"I agree."

"In the evening, let's take a walk along the shores of Lake Victoria, have fried fish and a coconut drink, and be grateful for life."

When evening came they found themselves on the shores of the lake walking side by side while holding hands, Oyunga shirtless and in shorts and Marion in a swimsuit and a loose, lace gown. Her stomach bulged out. They were talking, poking fun, and laughing loudly. In the distance, someone was watching them. A woman in a dark buibui. Lily.

CHAPTER 40

Closer Together

"You never told me how you got into this drug dealing bedlam?"

"Huh, not even a whisper?"

"I think I would remember a whisper that involved drugs."

"Well, I have always had these anxiety attacks. I think it's something to do with abandonment issues. They got worse as I grew older and hospital medication wasn't helping so I was introduced to someone who sold these special pills that took the attacks away."

"Lily?"

"Yeah, Lily. I became a regular customer and we started dating. At the time, I wasn't a chef yet and I needed some quick money and that's how I was sucked in.

At first, I enjoyed it because it was something novel, but then thoughts of the people who were being hurt started haunting me. The anxiety attacks got worse and the worse they got the more pills I took."

"And now?"

"Shouldn't you know the answer to that question? Aren't you with me all the time?"

"I don't know, sometimes you're with your cigarettes."

"Is that you being sarcastic? I thought that was my thing."

"I guess this is what they mean when they say someone is your rib, eh? You become part of their skin, you start behaving like them. One more month and I will be a fully functioning drug dealer."

They laughed heartily. They had just moved to Kisumu city. Oyunga was smoking less and he didn't need his special pills anymore. They were happy even though the day was gloomy. The sun had been swallowed behind dark clouds and there was a suffocating humidity in the air.

It had been over six months and even though Oyunga was conscious about the cartel tracing their money, he thought they were no longer on its radar. He needed somewhere Marion could run for checkups now that the twins were almost here. They also needed a modern house with amenities, a comfortable place with fewer mosquitoes than Ndukiya.

They had just unpacked and Oyunga was sitting on the couch, back from scouting buildings in which he was thinking of renting space.

"I think I can now go back to being a full-time chef. Thank you, Mari, for being patient with me."

"I didn't think I would grow to love you. I thought I'd

resent you every waking day but life has a way of surprising you."

"Are you still burning to go back to advertising?"

"I would like to go back to it but I guess I have to lay low. Maybe I can help you run the restaurant?"

"Mari, do you think we're being naïve?"

"Naïve?"

"Thinking they're not looking for us. Because every day I see a man in a suit or a man in a leather jacket or a light-skinned woman I think it's them."

"Tell me about it. I flinch every time I see a Noah but don't worry too much, they also have lives of their own to live."

"You don't know Lily. She's vengeful and spiteful. We have to be very careful. The restaurant we are opening; we have to run it behind the curtain. We can't be the face of it."

"Okay, whatever you say." Marion was completely lost in love and the babies growing in her stomach.

"Don't we have checkup today?"

"We do, but I can go by myself."

"No, no, you can't exclude me every time. I will take you today."

"Come on, honey, is that necessary? I can still drive just as good as you even with this protruding belly."

"I don't doubt that one bit," he grinned. "But allow me to be your chauffeur, if only for today, m'lady."

CHAPTER 41

Doctor's Appointment

OYUNGA PARKED THE car and helped Marion out. She now understood why they called pregnant women heavy. She was in an avocado green maternity dress and sandals and she walked slowly, stopping every two minutes to suck in air.

"Do you need help?"

"No, I'm fine, I just need a minute."

Oyunga took one of her arms and put it around his neck so that she leaned on him and he helped her inside the hospital.

"Two more months to go, how are you feeling?" the doctor said while putting on his gloves.

"Besides insomnia and feeling a bit heavy, I'm okay."

"Insomnia is quite common at this stage, especially with twins," he continued as he did the ultrasound. "Oh, look at that, your babies look very healthy. Looks like they're going to be happy and energetic little kids."

Oyunga was holding Marion's hand and they both grinned, their cheeks rosy with excitement.

"You continue eating iron, protein, and fiber-rich foods like we talked about and everything should be fine."

"Thank you, doc, I will personally see to that," Oyunga said.

They came out, Oyunga supporting Marion like he had done when they were going in. When they got close to their car, Oyunga stopped. Marion removed her arm from his shoulders as he felt his pockets in frenetic movements.

"What's wrong, honey?"

"I think I have left my phone in the hospital. Take the keys. I'll get you inside the car." Oyunga handed her the keys and made toward the hospital.

He had not gone ten steps when he heard a loud blast. Boom! He turned and put his hands on his head. Tiny bits of their Nissan Datsun flew in the air, which was now rich with thick, black smoke and bright, orange flames.

CHAPTER 42

Oyunga

OYUNGA WAS BREATHING HARD. His memory kept replaying the events like a broken record. He handed Marion the car keys then he turned around and saw the car fly into a flame of tiny pieces. In other instances, he saw himself saving Marion and his unborn twins from the explosion. Other times, Marion was the one saving him from the explosion. And yet in others, their son and daughter were the ones saving them.

He hiccupped and raced around the house like a madman. He knew it was the cartel. They wanted to kill them both, that was their plan. He cursed himself for not being inside the car so they could all die together. He ran to the bedroom, came back with a rope, and tied a noose on the ceiling fan. But when he tried to climb atop, the fan came tumbling down.

He untied the rope from the fan and got something sturdier. A metal ring on the side of the wall. But before he could ring his neck with the noose his phone buzzed. He looked at the screen. He had a new message:

Pity what happened to your baby momma. It's time to come back home, hon.

Oyunga looked at the text. The explosive the cartel used must have had a timer which Lily triggered when Marion entered the car. *She must be in town.* His entire being curdled with hatred for her. He wondered how she had gotten his new number. He looked at the noose on the wall and paced across the room one more time, everything suddenly clear. He had to avenge his love.

Dear Mari,

I still remember the first time we met. I remember your easy smile and your light soul. Your white dress, your short hair, and your loving manner. I'm sure you're in heaven, beautifying the place. We did not meet in the best circumstances but it started something beautiful. I remember how I longed for you. I longed for you the same way the Titanic longed for land and like the Titanic, I'm now here in a wreckage, sinking in a sea of my own making, with land nowhere in sight.

I know our kids would have been great people. I have no doubt that your love and care would have brought out the best in them. I'm sure they would have had your easy smile and your leadership verve. They wouldn't have been like me: vain, attracted to shiny things and quick fixes. They would have been more like you: smart, resilient, unwavering.

I'm here without all of you. The pain slices me into pieces every second. I guess it's the price I have to pay for my choices but I feel it's too big a price to pay. I don't know how to be strong and the only thing that is keeping me going is the thought of you. You were the very pillars that propped me up and made nothing seem like something.

I know what I'm about to do is not something you would advocate for. You, who wants me to give my mother a chance. The mother who abandoned me when I was a small pup. You, who stayed beside a drug dealer and gave him twins. I know you wouldn't want me to risk my life taking down the people who took you away from me but I must. I have to do this thing for our kids, for you, for us.

With Love,

Oyunga French

PART TWO

"When sorrows come, they come not single spies but in battalions." – King Claudius, Hamlet

CHAPTER 43

Lily

Lily picked up her phone from her king-size bed. It was the latest iPhone, unveiled less than a month ago. She eyeballed it and it unlocked automatically. She moved to the glass door and opened it. The cold breeze instantly made her nipples poke her silk nightgown.

She was staying in a five-star hotel overlooking Lake Victoria and the view was breathtaking. She admired it for a moment. In the distance, she could see fishermen in their canoes. Closer, she could see people exchanging chatter. She closed her eyes and wished for a moment that her life was that simple.

She closed the glass door, pulled back the curtain, and dialed The Scorpion. Today was not the day she wanted walls to have ears or eyes.

He picked on the second ring.

Only Lily had that kind of clearance. The rest of them had to go through all sorts of hoops before gaining access to him. She smiled and thought of giggling in a horny teenager sort of way and asking him how he was holding up without a human blanket, but she decided against it. The seriousness of the matter she was about to address required her to go straight to the point.

"Oyunga has been neutralized. I don't think he will be a problem anymore." She knew she had made a mistake with her wording immediately she mouthed the words.

"That's fantastic news, Quicksilver, but what do you mean, 'think'? Isn't it a done deal?" The voice at the other end was metallic, devoid of emotion.

"I am looking at the car his little love fling was in as we speak. It's been reduced to fragments," she said while moving the menu and the remote on her desk to keep her right hand busy. In a weird sense, it made her feel more anchored in the conversation, made her mind think a bit quicker. But even then she was no match for The Scorpion.

"Good. Oyunga wasn't in that car, was he?"

Lily thought about lying but then she reconsidered. She had known The Scorpion long enough to know that you could never bend a truth of such magnitude. The Scorpion would always find out and when he did there would be hell to pay.

"No, he wasn't," she said. Her tone was icy but The Scorpion felt the warmth in it.

"You realize he also has to go, don't you?"

"Is there a need for that? I can convince him back to our side."

"You just neutralized his woman and I have been made to believe that that woman was carrying his twins." He said 'made to believe' as if challenging Lily to tell him otherwise. He paused for a split second longer. "I don't think he will meet you with flowers. Neutralize him."

"We are to get married," Lily shrieked.

"Put that out of your mind. We can't afford a chink in our armor, or do I need to remind you which side of your bread is buttered?"

The Scorpion's word was usually final. Lily was the only one who could go back and forth with him. But she also knew when she was pushing the envelope a bit too far. She decided she would make it seem as if she was hunting down Oyunga when really, she would be using all her skills to try and bring him back to her side. Surely once The Scorpion saw his unwavering loyalty he would reconsider.

"Okay. Your wish, my command," she said and the line went dead.

She put on a coat and went lingerie shopping. She intended to use all of her skills to woo Oyunga back to her side.

CHAPTER 44

Oyunga

OYUNGA HAD JUST touched down in Nairobi. He had just had a sit-down with Marion's uncle. Her uncle had seemed concerned about Marion's death but Oyunga realized later that he had only been worried about spending his own money on the funeral.

When he heard her body had been blown to bits, instead of getting angry, he seemed to loosen up. He loosened up even further when Oyunga said he would foot the funeral bill. He needed him to gather Marion's relatives and pick a place on their ancestral land where she would rest. The uncle nodded in agreement after Oyunga handed him a wad of two hundred thousand bob for expenses.

His next destination was Marion's office. He looked at the exposed stone edifice she had worked in and wondered how he would broach the subject.

He was already feeling weak after the conversation with her uncle. Tears were knocking on his eyelids. He breathed in a chunk of snot and walked to the reception area.

"I'm here with a message about Marion, whom can I talk to?"

Immediately he said the name Marion the receptionist's eyes lit up.

"Oh, Marion, how is she? She was such an amazing boss. We did not understand why she wrapped up things so hurriedly. It wasn't her style at all."

"I'm afraid she is no longer with us," Oyunga said with his face to the floor. The receptionist understood immediately what he meant. Her face sagged and she got up.

"Come, the boss's office is this way."

Sandeep was seated at his desk in his Givenchy pinstripe suit. His feet were on top of his mahogany table and he was staring at the picture of his wife and two kids on the table. He was considering a divorce but did not know how it would rub off on the kids. He also didn't know how it would rub off on him. He was a man who had always had bouts of loneliness; a type of abyss that would leave him functionless without company. It suited him to have a wife or a longtime companion.

He looked at the photo again and this time instead of seeing his wife's face, he saw Marion's. He smashed the cigar he was smoking on an ashtray and reached for his Galaxy Note. He opened up the photo gallery to a picture of Marion. "Wherever did you go that is so top-secret, no contact of mine can seem to locate you?" he murmured into his bowtie while zooming in on her face, but before he could form a concrete thought, the door flew open.

"Someone is here to see you about Marion," the receptionist chirped.

He jumped out of his leather chair, feeling as if the fate of his second wife-to-be had come knocking on his door, but all those dreams dried up the second he saw the raw sadness on Oyunga's face.

He moved to the corner of his office, poured two fingers of whisky into a glass, dropped in two ice-cubes, and handed it to Oyunga. He then poured three fingers for himself and didn't reach for the ice-cube tray.

"How did she go?"

"A car explosion. It replays in my mind every night like some broken record."

"An accident?"

"No, foul play."

"You know the guys who did it?"

"Yes."

"You're going after them, aren't you?"

It wasn't framed as a question that needed an answer but Oyunga took it as one because he wanted to feel the anger froth up his mouth once more. He could now taste it on his tongue like copper.

"With everything I got."

"She was my favorite, you know," Sandeep said while walking him to the designated lounge area in his office. He sat in one corner of the brown leather sofa and crossed his legs. Oyunga sat on the other corner with his legs apart. "I used to see her and everything in me buzzed like a fridge that had been plugged in. Sometimes I didn't know what to do with myself when she walked in. She was something."

It was the first time that Oyunga let out the waterworks. It started with a lone tear running bereft on his left cheek after he blinked, followed by a mouthful of hiccups and then a gush of tears. Sandeep left him to it. He went to the table and came back with napkins.

"She was carrying my twins; I should have been in that car with her."

"Don't say such things. We need to get those guys. I have some contacts that might be useful. If you need anything all you have to do is give me a buzz."

"Her funeral is coming up; it would be great if her colleagues could be there."

"They used to adore her around here. You can count on them."

It was the first time in a long time that Oyunga had been vulnerable. Sandeep was an older gent and he had probably gone through his fair share of turmoil. *I needed this*, he thought while getting up and stretching out his hand to Sandeep.

"Thank you for your support. I will remember it."

"Let's get those bastards."

"They don't have a clue what's coming to them," Oyunga said while reaching for the door. The receptionist was not at her desk. He lingered for a second and imagined that the entire Nairobi must know that Marion had passed by now.

CHAPTER 45

Lily

THERE WAS A knock on the door. Lily was trying out her lingerie. She was in a see-through purple gown whose hem came to a halt slightly below her hips. Her nipples, dark and menacing against the contrast of her yellow skin, were exposed for the world to see. She looked risqué, like sex on legs. She didn't bother covering up with a robe. She went to her bedside and picked up her light compact revolver. She held it with ease, like you would hold a spoon or a piece of bread. She loved it. It almost looked like an ornament in her hand. She hid it from vision behind her back and opened the door.

"You're going to open the door for your husband with a gun, where has decorum gone to in this country?" Frankie said with a cheeky smile. The gold tooth in his mouth glinted in the yellow light in the room.

"Nobody told me you were coming," Lily said, amused. He let himself in and started checking out the place.

"Well, I had to come, judging by the way you are running amok up here. But turns out, it's a waste of a trip."

"What do you mean 'waste of a trip'?"

"Haha, nobody has told you? Your little pretty boy has checked back into Nairobi. He's making funeral arrangements for the little love thing of his you blew to bits. You're going to pay for that, you know. It's the one thing you have in common with that bastard. Vengeance. I hope you're prepared," he said, his physique close to her. His nostrils breathed her aura in. He ran his hands through her hair and Lily let him.

"It doesn't have to be a complete waste of a trip, you know."

"It doesn't," she said almost in a whisper. Frankie's right hand took the LCR from her left hand and placed it on the table then he used the same hand to squeeze her firm buttocks. Blood rushed from his head to his manhood and Lily's nipples stood erect.

"Before we go there, tell me what the plan is?" she breathed out a moan.

"We're going to hit him at the funeral. It's going down in Murang'a this weekend. My boys are already down there setting up camp. He will never see it coming."

Lily's arousal faded and she pushed away.

"At a funeral, come on, Frankie, even you are better than that. Let the man mourn, at least."

"Mourn? Haha. You're ridiculous, Quicksilver. It's one of the qualities I love most about you." He approached her but she moved back. "All of a sudden you have the moral high ground to decide where people should die? Hilarious. This one is going to be one for the record books. Like the Red Wedding, only grander." He smiled again and his gold tooth gleamed.

"Get out the same way you came in," she said irritated.

Lily knew that her best move would have been to act unbothered but she was overpowered with a rage that could only be informed by love. She did not understand how The Scorpion could expect her to be okay with him taking out her fiancé as if he were a household roach.

"I said get out." Her tone was rising.

"You look tired. I'm going to let you relax. Think things through. Get a clear mind and realize that this is going to be done one way or the other and the sooner you get on board, the better for us." He grabbed his manhood and winked at her while the door clicked behind him.

Lily opened the glass door. The soft breeze kissed her breasts and her nipples stood erect again. *No, not Oyunga.* She thought of the last time they shared a bed and her pulse raced.

She reached up her thigh and parted her lips. She was sticky. She stuck a finger and exhaled. She could have used Frankie's company if only he did not act a fool. She shoved another finger into herself. It did not do the trick. She moved away from the door and went to her bag. She was going to need something more powerful than two fingers.

CHAPTER 46

The Phone Call

THEY MOVED BRISKLY, not wanting to seem as if they were following him and at the same time trying to make sure they didn't lose him in the multitude of people in the market. They jumped over a vendor's groundnuts and almost stepped on someone's tomatoes. They breathed a sigh of relief when he finally broke away from the crowd and took an empty aisle to a warehouse that was selling coffins.

They looked at him select a snow-white coffin. "She was an angel," they heard him say and wondered if he was saying it because she really was an angel or because of the two hundred thousand bob Oyunga had given him that sat underneath his mattress.

They watched him hire a pick-up and followed him closely to the funeral home.

They returned later that night, entered the washrooms, and changed into green jumpsuits and dark gumboots. Exactly what the morticians at the morgue wore.

All that was left of Marion were fragments of bones, nothing much, but the undertaker had done his best to give her something of a face and a body, which was adorned in a dress. They opened the coffin and wired a kilo of C4 underneath the deceased's skull and in what was left of her legs. Anything an inch close to the casket would be obliterated. They smiled at their great work and dialed Frankie. His number was busy, tied up in a conversation with Lily.

"You were right. He has to go. Maybe this is God's way of giving us another chance," Lily sang, her voice two octaves lower, almost moaning into the phone.

"Uh, uh, uh. Look who has come to her senses. Are you going to sell out pretty boy that fast?" He used the words 'pretty boy' not necessarily to describe Oyunga's physical appeal but to mean he was a weakling.

"I spoke to The Scorpion." Frankie froze at the word and the power it wielded and the unique position it put Lily in before getting back into character. "It's going to be a test for me. He wants to see how unwavering my loyalty is. Frankie, give me the chance, eh, for old times' sake?"

"You will have to prove your unwavering loyalty another way, Quicksilver. My ass is on the line as much as yours is. Do you understand? The only bone I can throw you is, there's going to be C4, lots of C4, involved." The line went dead.

More than anything, Frankie wanted to show her who was in charge and at the same time put her on a short leash so that she had enough rope to know that the door was open for them to be what they once were, but not enough for her to hang him with it.

C4? That was too messy for her taste. She thought about the headlines, then she realized that Frankie probably had all the important journalists in his back pocket. And what were journalists but people, people with agendas: mouths to feed, a wife with needs, a girlfriend to romance? All you needed to do was throw a bit of money their way and they would dance to any tune that you played. They would say it was a transformer explosion, heck, they would say it was floods if that's what Frankie wanted them to write.

She packed her lime green bikini in her suitcase. She had actually thought that she would have a bit of time to sun-bathe in Takawiri beach, preferably with Oyunga in her arms. *C4*. The chemical kept jumping to her mind. But where, and how would she warn Oyunga without making it look as though she was a mole? A text? Her phone was probably bugged by now and her every move was being monitored. She thought of calling Frankie and begging. No, that was out of the question.

It came to her when her plane touched down at Wilson Airport. Frankie had mentioned that he had boys. People doing all the legwork for him. She only needed to look at the Shemeji Cartel database and pull their names up. She crossed her fingers and prayed that one of them was overindulgent. In a carnal pleasure sort of way.

CHAPTER 47

The Roach

HE HAD THOUGHT he would be a boxer. He was built for it–a tank on legs–but his dad had wanted him to be an accountant. That's why he had dragged him to his insurance company until he realized it was a lost cause. His dad was fine with him being a dunderhead with no brain for numbers but what he couldn't stomach were his other preferences. The last thing his dad wanted was his name soiled.

All the same, his dad opened a cyber café for him because his other preferences did not make him any less his son, although there were days he wished they would. Martin thought how ridiculous that idea had been. A cyber café? What did his father expect him to do with damn computers? He sold all of them and used the money to go to boxing bouts and to romance the many boys in Nairobi who were in the closet.

Zero had approached him after seeing him fighting in a boxing bout with a rage devoid of humanity. At the time, he had burnt all his money and he was flat on his back. Zero told him he had a job for him as a personal bodyguard, as his executioner. He took it with his broad shoulders open. "Of course, I don't expect you to make any moves on me." It was those words that made him understand that Zero knew his sexual orientation and that he was okay with it. It was also in that way that they developed a friendship that went far beyond work.

He now sat at the counter of one of the many restaurants in Murang'a, in his hand a glass of brandy. He thought about his wife, Prisca. In a way, she had salvaged him. His family looked at him not with loathing but with dignity. But she had also pushed him further away from his truth and he resented her for that. He tried taking his mind off his pregnant wife by eyeballing the screen. It was showing a rerun of Floyd Mayweather versus Manny Pacquiao.

At the corner of the restaurant, Lily was watching him behind dark sunglasses. You couldn't have said that she was the femme-fatale that made men fall head over heels. She was in a grey jumper, dark pants, and white socks that slid inside flip flops, her wisps of hair hidden behind a cap. She looked like those women who had let themselves go and no man with a shred of dignity had any business talking to them.

She watched as her accomplice walked in. A thin, nimble man in a grey muscle shirt, a blue denim jacket, skinny jeans, and on his feet, shining, brown leather shoes.

"What a poor showing that boxing match was," he said, his voice clear and mellow like white wine.

Martin searched him from head to toe and sneered. It said that he approved of what he saw.

"Tell me about it, I was almost falling asleep watching it," he responded. Not only had he liked what he saw, he was also turning on the charm. It was rare for The Roach to make humor. His style of communication was silence followed by action.

"A hugging contest if I were asked." Josh was one of those people who had been living in the closet his entire life but he always found himself getting into frivolous activities. He was a very sober accountant in a respected company by day but by night he liked to get into debauchery. Lily had stumbled upon him the same way she had stumbled upon Oyunga.

When she called him to ask for a favor, he was all fireworks and disco lights. Especially after he saw The Roach's profile; all muscle and that scar on his face that made him look dangerous. He accepted the job with glee. For him, it was an adventure.

The Roach searched his face. It was docile. Harmless. One of those common faces that gives you a sense of security, even though you should be wary because it was such faces that got into the most treachery.

"What's your poison?"

"I will have a gin and tonic or any drink with an umbrella." Josh knew exactly the kind of game they were playing. The Roach liked to be dominant and in charge and Josh, well, he loved being dominated.

"Or we can just have that gin and tonic in my hotel room?"

"Come on, at least buy me lunch first?"

The Roach smiled. He had actually taken it literally. "Well, it's evening so that would be supper."

Josh knew he had to move quickly, the funeral was set

for the morrow. Lily had not gotten into the gory details but she had told him that it would all be in vain if he was successful a day later.

"Where is your hotel room?"

"It's at the Fairmont."

"Whoa, your boss spares no expense, eh? Or do you work for yourself?"

"I don't like talking about work. It's the quickest way to get me into a mood."

"I wouldn't mind fresh blankets and room service."

They jumped into a taxi and before it clocked midnight, Lily had photos of the room. She had told him to take photos of everything: the wardrobe, the shower, the inside of bags, anything that would be telling.

This wasn't easy, this man doesn't sleep, you make a movement and he's up. I hope this is enough.

At least tell me the sex was good?

Josh replied with the smiling devil emoji.

Lily opened the photos. The bed was unmade and on one side The Roach seemed to be asleep. Even while sleeping he looked deadly, like a loaded gun with the hammer pushed back. There was a small safe beside the bed and a bag that Josh had probably dragged out of somewhere and opened. Inside the bag were what looked like five grenades, two M16s, and one bulletproof vest. Sequestered in between them was a detonator. She wondered if they planned to storm the funeral mass at the church and start blasting, or whether they planned to do it at the grave.

No, Frankie might not be smart but he was not all that dumb. He wouldn't want his best men to be identified. If she had seen sniper rifles, that would have been a different case. Lily also knew Frankie's style. His feeling was that when one person was contaminated, everybody around him was also contaminated and he believed it was his job to wipe them all out. What was the one place those close to Oyunga would be? That was the question that needed an answer.

Explosives, she thought again. Are they going to hurl grenades at the mass? That has too much of a margin of error. *C4? Detonator?* It came to her almost in a split second. Oyunga and all his loved ones would probably be seated in the front row. *They are going to wire the front seats with explosives and trigger it from a safe house,* she thought. She got onto her Kawasaki Supersport and headed to the church in the dark of night.

Oyunga

OYUNGA LOOKED DAPPER in his dark suit. It matched his melancholy. He had just disembarked from the car that was carrying the hearse. It was a glossy, dark car that almost resembled a limousine. He was shaking hands with and giving thanks to Sandeep who was in an equally dark suit and a grey bowtie that matched the silver in his hair.

He went ahead and thanked the colleagues who had shown up, shook their hands then moved swiftly to Marion's family. The uncle had put in more work than he thought he would. "This was our little girl, only the best for her," he said in that way that a person who wants to prove himself says.

Marion's friend, Prisca, was also there. Her stomach was outward and protruding. Oyunga expected the pregnancy to give her face a glow but instead, she looked emaciated and tired, with streaks of black patches beneath her left eye and on her upper lip.

"Hi, Prisca, how are you?"

"I'm pregnant. It's really sad what happened, how are you holding up?"

"I'm trying. It's a bit easier with all the support I'm getting."

"I was told it was a car explosion?"

"Yes, the gear jammed. I really blame myself." Oyunga did not feel the need to get into details.

"Well. I have to leave now. For some reason, my husband wants me home before noon."

"Take care and have some rest. If not for you, for the baby."

Oyunga had half a smile as he watched her get into a taxi. He had heard all sorts of stories about her husband. He reminded himself that it was none of his business. He was glad she had come to pay her respects even with her protruding belly. For a moment the melancholy ebbed at the thought but then it struck him again like a hammer when they called the people who were close to the deceased to come and carry the coffin into the church.

CHAPTER 49

The Muscle

IN A CAFÉ next to the church were seated The Roach and Zero, having coffee as if it were another normal day. The Roach was in baggy trousers, a loose shirt, and slippers. Zero was in shorts, a vest, and on top of it, a v-neck sweater. He was eyeballing the newspaper. He was reading a story about a gunslinger who was arraigned in court for murder.

"Can you believe this?"

"What?"

"Look at the headline."

The Roach stared as if the newspaper was made of clear glass.

"It's like we're living in a banana republic, eh? You can be walking down the streets and, BOOM, your life is snapped in a split second. Savages."

The waitress, a short, voluptuous woman with heavy breasts and thick thighs brought an omelet and two sausages for Zero. Zero was one of those people who could eat anything and everything and his physique never changed. She had a glass of mango juice for The Roach.

"You look well relaxed. Did you see someone besides your wife last night?" He was now searching The Roach's face, unleashing all of his intelligence on him, all the psychology and human nuances he had learned in varsity doing criminology. The Roach knew he couldn't lie to him.

"I had a bit of a tryst last night."

"You were careful?"

"Yeah, yeah. I checked out his profile. An accountant in one of those Weetabix organizations every child wants to work for."

"A one-time thing?"

"Yeah, sure."

"Keep it that way, the last thing we need is another distraction."

"Is the duck ready to cluck?" The Roach asked, changing topics.

"They should be getting into mass right now. Has your wife left?"

"Yes, she just texted. Arm it, let the duck cluck while they escort it to church so we can be done and dusted by noon."

"What's the hurry for? You want to go back to your accountant, eh, lover boy? Give them time. Let them do their speeches and then when they least expect it, KABOOM."

The Roach sneered. "She's going to die twice. Poor thing."

Zero looked at the memorial card in front of him. The

mass was scheduled to be done in two hours' time. Songs from the choir, speeches from the Women's Guild, speeches from loved ones, speeches from close friends, prayers afterward. He got exhausted just by looking at it. But he was happy to see that Oyunga, Sandeep, and the uncle were all on the roster.

"They should be carrying the coffin or they should be at least somewhere close to it."

He smiled, removed the detonator from his pocket, and armed it for two hours forty-five minutes. He knew that people were never on time, not on this side of the Sahara at least. It started counting down and he got back to his newspaper.

"Jeez, what is this country coming to when someone can walk down the streets and shoot an innocent person. Christ."

CHAPTER 50

Oyunga

HER UNCLE WAS the last one to speak. Oyunga was surprised to see tears trickle down his cheeks.

The service was scheduled to start at 10:00 am and end at noon. Oyunga looked at his watch when the final prayers were made and family and close friends were ushered forward to carry the coffin. The clock read 12:41 pm.

Sandeep and Oyunga held the coffin from the front. The uncle and a cousin were in the middle. Oyunga's friend, Arigula, and one of Marion's colleagues were at the back. Sandeep told them to hold on for a second as he removed the cufflinks on his cream shirt and went on to fold it to arm's length then held the coffin with a fine grip. His golden wedding ring created a perfect contrast with the milk-white coffin.

The pastor in charge of the ceremony got in front of the coffin with his hymn book and led the entire congregation in song as Oyunga and company, a step at a time, sang. The clock ticked and tocked.

135

CHAPTER 51

Uninvited Guest

OYUNGA HAD PUT up a great performance at the church. The waterworks had not come. But now as he stood at the grave watching the coffin being lowered by electric motors, the tears came effortlessly. He insisted on looking. He had to see the coffin going down. He had to feel the pain. He needed all the pain he could gather to build up enough anger to go after the people that had done this.

He picked up a shovel and started throwing in the sand as the pastor chimed, "Sand shall return to sand and soil to soil. We are only here for a short while and we should make good use of it as best we can." Oyunga's vision blurred with tears and mud because he kept rubbing his nose with the back of his hand, the same hand which was full of soil. It was Arigula who took the shovel away from him because he kept throwing soil on top of the already covered grave, creating a small hill.

"It's done, my brother, it's done. She's resting now," Arigula said while taking away the shovel.

Oyunga lifted himself. Almost everyone was crying; even Sandeep who had been so composed had his face covered up with a handkerchief.

He was also around, the shadow of a figure, in his usual lowered hat so that you only saw parts of his nose and his mouth. Immediately Oyunga saw him he knew something was up.

CHAPTER 52

Lily

LILY HAD GOTTEN to the church frantic. Her knickers in knots. She had checked all the seats and there was no sign of explosives. She was starting to get restless. It would be the first time that Frankie had outwitted her. She felt shame at the thought of it. *Think Lily, think. 'Explosives' is what he said. He might have been leading you on.*

She went back to the phone and scrolled through the images again, this time slowly, carefully, using the trained eyes of a woman who was hot on the trail of a cheating husband. She looked at the unmade bed again and The Roach sleeping in it. She searched his unconscious face for clues. There were none.

She moved her eyes back to the bag and carefully looked at the M16's, grenades, bulletproof vest, and the detonator. She was back to where she had started.

She moved her gaze carefully. On the desk were condoms, a remote control, and a bottle of mineral water. In the shower were soap and towels, just what you would expect in a functional bathroom.

She brushed through the wardrobe photos. She looked back again and saw the clothes, regalia to the workers at the coroner. Her eureka moment came almost instantly. *They wired the body with explosives and nobody will see it coming. The body was so badly damaged that even bags of C4 might seem like prosthetics to reconstruct the body,* she thought.

It was almost approaching morning when she got to the funeral home. The guard on duty was fast asleep. Not even the sound of her Kawasaki Supersport could wake him up.

Two wires inside the padlock and it was open. A few master keys and she was looking at what was supposed to be Marion's body. It was dressed and ready for the big day. There were no signs of explosives. "Did Frankie grow another set of brains while I was away?" she wondered.

She walked across the room three times while trying to think and then she decided that the coffin had to be the play, there was no other angle. She decided to look at it again, more carefully this time just in case she had missed something like before.

She saw it when she was almost giving up. A small chip, hidden underneath the femur. It would just give the detonator on the other end a signal that the explosive was armed, but the explosive could not do any harm.

Someone had been here after Frankie's goons had left. Someone who disarmed the bomb and who was clever enough to set up the decoy. She knew for a fact that it couldn't be Oyunga's work. He wasn't that skilled but it seemed he had friends who were.

She put the body back the way she had found it and slipped out of the funeral home. The guard on duty was still snoring.

CHAPTER 53

Frankie

THE TENSION IN the room could be dressed in a suit and attend an event. Frankie had just thrown a chair into the flat-screen TV of the hotel room. The only thing that could appease him at the moment was shooting someone point-blank in the face, but who?

"Tell me, how is it possible that this bastard keeps running rings around us? Zero, you're supposed to be the brains of this entire operation. Are you saying that you can no longer do your job?"

"Boss, everything was done according to plan. Someone must have thwarted our efforts. What about Quicksilver?"

It was known that Lily and Frankie were close. Without so many words, Zero was suggesting that something may have slipped during these close moments.

"What are you saying, that I gave Lily my plans? Give me clear answers or there will be hell to pay."

"He must be working with someone; he must have a lookout."

"You know what I'm hearing? I'm hearing that your operation has a mole and you're trying to cover up for them," he said while holding Zero by the collar. "What I want is a timesheet of all your activities from the time you wired the explosive to the time it supposedly went off. If you took a piss. I want it on the timesheet. If you went out to buy a packet of condoms, I want it on the timesheet. Heck, if you came back and made an omelet let it be on the goddamn timesheet."

He picked up his Glock and jacket while Zero smoothed out the wrinkles on his shirt.

"I will be expecting a call from you, you better have results." Frankie kicked a table next to the door with his combat boot and stormed out.

CHAPTER 54

Josh

HAD YOU TOLD Josh today was the day he would die, he wouldn't have believed you. He woke up like he usually did, with a black pad over his eyes and earmuffs on his head. He loved his beauty sleep. He got up in his pink pajamas and went to the toilet to take a piss. He did it while sitting, his face stuck on his iPhone. He was scrolling through Instagram, looking at the many male models he fancied. He double-tapped the photos, 'mmh's and aah's,' escaping him. "Looks like today is going to be a sunny day," he said. It rained torrents later that afternoon.

He went to the kitchen and made a coffee then spread peanut butter and honey on brown bread. He had always felt peanut butter was a healthier alternative to margarine. He sat down on his flowery sofa, not wanting to think about work. If he stared at another excel sheet his eyeballs would pop.

The funny thing was that he was good at it. And he was rising meteorically in his job. Very soon he would have saved enough to leave the job and live the way he wanted. He laughed at the thought because all his money disappeared in concerts and expensive vacations. Another chunk went to clothes. Living a glamorous life was not easy.

He put his coffee away and started filing his nails, gently blowing them after every second. It felt greatly therapeutic. He had maybe an hour to kill before he would start preparing for work. It was during this activity of filing and blowing his nails that there was a knock on his door. The Roach was on the other side.

"What a fantastic surprise! You know I was thinking of skipping work today and now I have the perfect excuse. What is that, is that a cold I'm developing?" Josh said after letting him in.

"I'm sorry, Josh, this is not that kind of visit," The Roach said with an icy tone, reeling that Josh had set him up.

"What do you mean?" Josh's voice was trembling. Immediately The Roach had spoken he had known this was about the photos he took. He thought about how naïve he had been, that he had not thought of the threat, not once. He had been too blinded by the needs of his flesh to think of his safety.

"It was a woman. Petite, extremely light skin. She goes by the name Mel but I suppose that is her pseudonym, isn't it?"

The Roach immediately knew it was Lily.

"What did she want with you?"

"Just photos. You don't have to catch a feeling about this, man. We had fun, didn't we? It can be our thing."

The Roach locked the door and started walking towards

Josh. Josh retreated. His legs knocked the arm of his flowery sofa and he fell on his back. The Roach picked up a lemon green cushion and pressed it down on Josh's face. Josh's sphincter let loose and he defecated. It was the only part of him that did not smell flowery.

CHAPTER 55

Prisca

THE BABY CAME, screaming and bouncing. A girl who resembled her parents in every way. She had Prisca's big, brown eyes, and even with her fat cheeks, you could tell that she was going to have high cheekbones just like her mom. When she started giggling, her smile came out like that of her dad, endearing, and icy.

Seeing they had created something in their image heightened their attraction and it brought them together, if only for a while. Martin minimized his late nights to help with the baby. He even made love to her even though it was awkward. His manhood kept going soft. Prisca thought it was because she had just given birth. She hoped that his libido would return once her womanhood snapped back.

They called her Grace because she had given their marriage a new form. Prisca and Martin's parents had new hope and were bent out of shape with the excitement of becoming first-time grandparents. The baby's maiden name was Njeri, the same as Prisca's mother to honor their side of the family.

The two sides of the family became friends of sorts. They would regularly drop by to visit and to teach the newlyweds one or two things about child care: how to change diapers and feed and clothe the tot. Prisca's father stopped looking at Martin the way he looked at him, as if he was an enemy, as if he was out to cause harm, not only to his daughter but also to the state, and started looking at him as a son-in-law.

CHAPTER 56

Oyunga

"You want to assassinate the Vice President of the Republic of Kenya. You know I had always thought you were a bit nuts but not this nuts," The Ghost said, his eyes covered from sight by his hat.

"He is the key to the end of this madness. Lily and Frankie can follow but you know he has to go," Oyunga said, lolling on his chair without the slightest clue of what it would take to accomplish what he was proposing.

"Let's say by some miracle you manage to get his schedule. How do you get close to him with his security detail swarming around him?"

"What about a sniper rifle?"

"Where will you position yourself? All buildings within a mile's radius are scanned and guarded."

"I'm not saying it's impossible but we don't have enough pieces or muscle at this point in our operation to go after The Scorpion. It would be a suicide mission."

"What do you suggest? A manhunt for me is on. If I don't get to them first they will get to me."

"I say we understand their operation first. Know who is in charge of what. Know who is Second-in-Command to The Scorpion. Who is third, fourth, fifth? Where they stay. Do they have wives, kids? What are their vulnerable points?"

"We don't do anything to wives and kids."

"We won't but you will be surprised what great pressure points they can be when it comes to making people cooperate. And we need that now more than anything. How much money do you have left?"

"About eight million, give or take."

"You wired it into the secure account I told you?"

"Yeah."

"Good, it will help us hire a black hat. Someone trustworthy who can hack their systems; texts, emails, the works. I know they might not convey important information through the internet because of its capricious nature but we need the little we can get. We need to know the security around them, political rallies that they have scheduled, boardroom meetings that they may be attending. That's how we get a hold of the top man."

CHAPTER 57

The Scorpion

THE TOP MAN sunk into his throne of a chair. He was in a simple, blue shirt, on top of it a brown jacket, and black trousers. He looked like any ordinary man–a supervisor in a restaurant or a manager in a supermarket–but there was something about him that made you afraid. His face exuded power and influence. His brown eyes were drilling into the people sitting in front of him. Frankie and Lily.

Frankie started speaking after the uneasiness of the silence in the room overwhelmed him. He would much rather quicken his fate, know how the chips would fall, than wallow in anxiety. He got up to speak.

"From my end, it is clear why the duck did not cluck."

He looked at Lily. She was in a flimsy, low-cut blouse, no bra. Her chest made a V from the base to her neck which had an emerald necklace around it. She was in a mini skirt but with her seated, it looked like a handkerchief.

Her feet sunk into red high heels. She crossed her legs and looked at Frankie and for a minute he wanted to change his story. But his life depended on it and he happened to love it more than he did Lily's legs.

"Quicksilver sent a mole to save her fiancé. The mole is at the bottom of the ocean as we speak." He shifted his weight from one leg to the other. "But I think it's clear now why the duck refused to cluck. If there are any steps to be taken, I will leave it to you." He made a small bow and took his seat.

"Is that all?" The Scorpion asked almost in a whisper but his voice reverberated across the room.

Frankie nodded then looked at Lily. She wore a poker face.

The Scorpion leaned to the far edge of his desk, picked up a yellow file, and threw it onto Frankie's lap.

"Have a look at that because it seems you have been living in a cave."

Frankie looked at the images of a man who was more of a shadow. Everything about him was concealed except his nose and mouth.

"I am made to understand that this is the same man who was the hero the night you were unable to get a hold of Oyunga's flame? I'm also made to understand he is the same man who neutralized your duck. Do you know anything about this?"

Frankie sat there open-mouthed.

"You are supposed to be the muscle of this operation, yet your genius move is trying to frame your partner?"

Frankie made to talk.

"Save it. I want information in regards to that man. Who is he? Who does he work for? Who has he worked for before? What does he know? His name? How does he look like?"

He raised his chin a bit to tell Frankie that he was dismissed. Frankie got up sore and left The Scorpion with Lily.

CHAPTER 58

Lily

"I KNOW I HAVE given this assignment to Frankie," The Scorpion spoke. "But we know you are the brains of this operation. Frankie has always been more muscle than mind. I want you to track this man. I have a bad feeling about him. He might know too much."

The Scorpion was right. That man was more dangerous than they thought and it was him and not Oyunga that they should have been worrying about.

Lily licked her lips, making the gloss on them shine a bit more.

"Of course you can count on me."

She smiled a wry smile. She had just reaffirmed her loyalty to the Shemeji Cartel and made Frankie look like an utter fool. All without the two of them knowing that she also had a separate manhunt for Oyunga, though hers was engineered by love.

She didn't think for a second that she was also in danger, chasing Oyunga. She still felt it was a relationship feud that could be resolved with a kiss.

She removed the thought from her mind. There were other, more pressing issues and she was looking at one of them. The Scorpion had gotten up and his trousers were bulging. His zip looked as if it would let rip any second now. Lily pushed her chair back and uncrossed her legs. She wasn't wearing any knickers.

CHAPTER 59

Oyunga

OYUNGA WAS IN grey shorts and a blue t-shirt. He was hopping on one leg while removing sand from his flip flops. It felt like tiny needles jarring his skin. He was starting to think that maybe the beach was not for him.

He had been on their trail for over an hour now, trying as much as possible to blend in without being noticed. The girl would make different poses and the man with a potbelly and a head that looked as black as tar would take photos.

Oyunga wondered why such an old man, and a respected Senator for that matter, would dye his otherwise white hair black but then he glanced at the thing he was taking photos of and understood why. She had a baby face, as if she was fresh from campus. Small breasts and a big behind. She seemed restless, jumping from one side of the beach to the other. Posing this way and that. Throwing up signs with her fingers and pouting every now and again.

Perhaps the Senator would get a heart attack trying to keep up with her and he would make his work easier, Oyunga thought with a smile.

He was in Zanzibar to collect intel and so far all he had gotten were blisters in between his toes and a sticky back from the heat. He needed a shower badly but he could not afford to look away from the lovely couple, not even for a second.

He gave them another look. They were odd, as if it was a father-daughter date, only the creepy father kept calling his daughter with one finger and kissing her on the mouth. There could have been tongue involved but Oyunga was not close enough to confirm that.

Some things disturbed Oyunga. He wondered what kind of stories such a girl fed her family when she went home driving a car that even people on a fourth job could not afford. But before he could finish that thought he saw the Senator breaking away from the girl. He had started to think the little young thing accompanied him everywhere. Oyunga waited until he was about fifteen paces away and approached her.

"Hi, what is a lovely girl like you doing out here all alone?"

She looked at him and Oyunga realized she was about to tell him she was with someone.

"Pardon my manners, I'm sure you have been called lovely a bunch of times. Ridiculously gorgeous is the word I was looking for," he said with a confident smile.

She smiled back and her body, which had started to tense up, relaxed.

"I'm Oyunga, a chef, doubling as a tourist. Maybe you can show me around?"

"I'm Claire," she said, all teeth now. She had missed the charms of a young man and even she prayed that her sponsor took a while longer to get back. Oyunga was busy searching their paraphernalia with his eyes, wondering where their hotel keycard was.

"So, Claire, tell me, what else are you into, besides taking selfies and looking ridiculously gorgeous?" He said it with a tone that should have made her take offense but she was now trying to impress him. She giggled. "I swim, do a bit of movie watching," she said while playing with her hair. She realized that Oyunga wasn't impressed and went for the ace. "I also attend wine tasting events."

"Huh, wine tasting events? Is that a thing? What kind of wine do you taste in these events?"

"White wine, umm and I think your toe is bleeding."

"Oh, this tourist is not that good at being a tourist, especially with the sand here being sharper than a scalpel."

"I have wet wipes. Here, it will clean the wound." She gave him the bag of wipes. The keycard was sequestered next to her lipstick."

She went ahead and put the open bag between them.

"The ocean is beautiful, isn't it, Claire? The way the waves are breaking in the distance." By the time she turned her neck Oyunga had taken the keycard and returned the bag of wipes.

"Yes, it is very romantic."

"You know what, Claire, it was nice to meet you but I better get going. Put this toe in ice before it falls off."

"Oh, that soon?"

Come on, don't pretend you're going to miss me."

She giggled.

"Just in case you do I'm in room three. I have this wine

bottle and no wine opener and I suppose someone seasoned in winery like you wouldn't lack such a tool hidden somewhere." He stared at her chest and winked. That was enough distraction for him to disappear into the throng of people with the keycard.

CHAPTER 60

Lily

LILY SAT IN her apartment in Mombasa. The apartment that was supposed to be her matrimonial home with Oyunga. She was in black underwear and slippers. She walked around, thinking about The Ghost. She wondered if she needed a team of maybe two to help her with things. All it would take was a whisper to The Scorpion and it would be done but then she thought against it. Hers was a lean operation, a one-woman outfit, and that is what made it work. In any case, she had all the weapons she needed. A brain, perfectly round breasts, and a hot pocket between her legs. This was a man's world and she had everything she needed to bring them to their knees.

She thought of The Ghost again. This was no ordinary man. Even The Scorpion thought he might be a problem and therein lay her first clue.

The Ghost had to have been in the Shemeji Cartel and not as a messenger or janitor; he must have had a high rank. Something like the head of security or the Second-in-Command to the very top. He must know the ins and outs of the cartel. The structure, the weakest link. He had it in him to make the cartel go belly up. If there was a list of Shemeji foes that needed elimination, he was at the very top of it.

She allowed herself to daydream for a second. If she were to bring The Ghost's head on a platter to The Scorpion the reward would be substantial and the trust immense. He might even turn a blind eye to the Oyunga menace. She decided that even as she tried to convince Oyunga, a full-blown manhunt for The Ghost would be on.

She started by calling their top techie. This was the man in charge of everything computer-related. If someone was trying to hack them, he knew. If people were exchanging salacious messages on texts, he knew. She reminded herself that she should pay him a visit. She wouldn't want such a man to be her enemy.

She started by asking for the database of all the ex-Shemeji Cartel members who had been eliminated. There was nothing like retiring from the cartel, you simply disappeared. She made a special request and asked him to narrow it down to high ranking agents. After thirty minutes she got a ping on her phone. She blew up the pdf document on her iPad Pro and started going through it.

There was Mshashiri. He had been the Secretary-General and the Second-in-Command. Tall, average build, with a face that could sell you a stone when you were hungry. A big consignment was coming in and he figured he could get away with it and start his operation. He was neutralized in the dunes of Saudi Arabia by the same people he was negotiating with.

There was Lumumba. Short, stalky, built like a rhinoceros. Chief executive of a blue-chip company and the Fifth-in-Command. He had a wife and a teenage son. The wife had discovered the ruinous activity he was involved in and she gave him an ultimatum. He told her he just needed time and it would all disappear. He chartered a private jet with plans to leave it all behind and disappear to Australia. He was neutralized before he got to the airport. His wife's and teenage son's bodies were found lifeless in the cockpit.

She emailed Oyunga the document on an anonymous line just to scare him. Then she went on flipping the document. Most of the victims had dull deaths. Trying to steal, trying to get away from it all. A loved one trying to have them see the light before it all came crashing down. The info started regurgitating itself and her eyelids started growing heavy until one, in particular, piqued her interest.

Marcus. Tall, dark, and slender, Minister of Defense and the head of security for the cartel. No wife, no kids. At least not according to the records she was looking at. His was a short paragraph. Cause of death: a helicopter crash in the Mara, his remains were never recovered. There were two photos of him. One from head to toe in which he was in a grey suit, standing in true general fashion. If he were shorter he would have resembled Putin. He had the look for it too, cold and calculating. The other was a passport-style photo. Even in a photo, those eyes bored into her and they reminded her of someone she knew. Could this be The Ghost? She put her phone aside and breathed a heavy sigh.

CHAPTER 61

Oyunga

OYUNGA SWIPED THE card to the presidential suite of the hotel. The Senator was sparing no expense in enticing the little young thing. He hid from the glare of the surveillance cameras with a low hanging cap and room service attire.

On his hands were a pair of gloves, specially designed to pick up fingerprints. The Ghost had informed him that the security was biometric, mostly fingerprint-based, because it was better encrypted. Iris and face scanners worked but they were too capricious, seeing as they were new technology.

He located the safe and true to The Ghost's word, it was fingerprint encrypted. So was the latest MacBook lying on the table, beside a glass of water. He looked at it against the light and saw the faintest trace of a fingerprint. He turned it to locate the forefinger and placed his directly on top of it. Then he headed to the safe. It buzzed and blinked red. Two more tries and it would trigger an alarm.

Next to the bed, on the nightstand, was a bible. Black, King James Version. He held the edges, dimmed the lights, and shone his blue ray torch on it. On the spine, he located the forefinger print and placed his on top of it. He placed it on the safe and it clicked open. *Huh, so he's a Jesus-loving son of a bitch, who'da guessed?*

Inside was a wad of cash, documentation, and blueprints to high-rising buildings. He took them, spread them on the little desk next to the glass of water and took photos then returned them.

He went to the laptop but before he could open it he decided to have a look out the window. He had a view of the entire beach. He saw them arguing while coming towards the hotel and he knew what the subject of the argument was. He removed his hard disk, opened the laptop, and started copying the drive on it. It was forty percent copied when they entered the hotel.

CHAPTER 62

Lily

"TELL ME ABOUT the Minister of Defense? The one that died in a helicopter crash in the Mara," Lily chirped while lying lazily on her side of the bed. The Scorpion had just put on his trousers and was buckling his belt.

"He never really died. He simply disappeared."

"And the helicopter crash?"

"It was a decoy. We couldn't have people in the Shemeji Cartel thinking that one of our own outfoxed us."

"Ten years is a long time."

"Yes, it's a long time. I was Third-in-Command at the time. I don't need to tell you that the second now sleeps with the fishes and the one who was the first holds the highest seat in the land."

"How good was he?"

"He was the best. He knew the ins and outs of the business but he didn't feel the First-in-Command should have the highest seat in the country. Let's just say he had morals and he started helping the opposition and he had to be let go."

"Only he's at large?"

"And that's why I am reopening Operation Mongoose. He was a fool going against the cartel and he's going to come to a fool's end."

CHAPTER 63

Oyunga

OYUNGA SAT IN his room replaying what had happened as if it were a movie. He had found them at the reception haggling and shouting at each other over who had lost the keycard. He had slipped it into the lady's big bag and as he turned he heard the Senator telling her to check it again.

"I have already checked a thousand times, what good will it do this time?" she asked while going through the bag. She sounded like an errant kid. The kind whose parenting was done through money and gifts. She smiled, embarrassed, when she found it.

Oyunga had gone to the washrooms, changed out of the room service regalia, and he now sat in his room feeling like a seasoned FBI special ops agent. He didn't enjoy this feeling for long before there was a knock on his door, behind it was Little Miss Voluptuous.

"Hi," she said. "Here is the wine opener you requested."

She was in a long, dark coat but underneath it was a purple see-through chemise. A part of him wanted to tell her to come in. It had been a long day and finding out what was underneath that chemise would have probably helped him unwind but he was here for surveillance and intel, not romance. A distraction was the last thing he needed.

"You've come at a bad time. My wife and two kids have just checked in."

"Oh, I'm truly sorry," she said, embarrassed. She handed him the opener, tightened the buckle on her coat, and disappeared into the corridors.

Oyunga went back to his bed and felt instantly sad. It is something they would have broken into laughter at if Marion had not been taken from him. He opened his laptop and got to work. His anger recharged.

CHAPTER 64

Arigula

THEY WERE AT Lake Bogoria taking images that would be used on the calendars of prestigious companies. The money had been better than he had anticipated and the job gave him a high like no other but now he wanted to push the envelope. He wanted to branch out and use his camera, not just for beauty but to solve problems. *A hero with a lens,* the thought flew into his head and he smiled.

He now found himself admiring photojournalists who were posted to places like Afghanistan, getting the chance to snap things that meant something. Things that could turn the world on its head.

His specialty was portraits. There was a way that he played with light and shadows that breathed life into his images; made them seem as if they were dancing to a tune. As if they were telling a secret. It was this that got him contracts from big brands and local and international celebrities.

He had taken a photo of a celebrity at the sunset of his years who later passed on. The photo was celebrated everywhere because at first glance it looked as if he was angry then at another glance he looked mellow and at peace. That photo drove the public nuts and made him an overnight sensation.

He still needed to supplement his income by taking up regular assignments but it was no problem for him. He did not go out looking for jobs. They came looking for him and he loved every second of it. He loved it: his ever-piling online audience, the attention he got even when he said something as mundane as 'The sky is blue.' But he didn't love all that as much as he loved the women in his private messages, groveling to him and throwing their knickers at his face.

He needed to maintain that high. He thought of Oyunga and all the mystery around him and decided that he should pay him a courtesy visit.

CHAPTER 65

Frankie

FRANKIE WAS RUNNING round in circles. His first move was getting the surveillance footage close to Kilimani the day his men were chasing Oyunga's flame. He managed to get the plates of the sedan The Ghost was driving but on trying to locate it on the government database, it did not exist. That was his first dead end.

The second one came after he sent his muscle to Murang'a to ask questions around the funeral home. Most people were clueless. *This man was supposed to be close to Oyunga. He could be a relative, a close friend, or an acquaintance,* he thought. His next ace was to pull up the records of everyone Oyunga worked closely with but nothing matched the profile of The Ghost.

Time was running out and he didn't have a clue who this shadow of a person was. He finally threw in the towel and gave Lily a call.

"Hello, Sugar, how's life treating you?"

"Not very well after you threw me under the bus the other day. I thought we were compadres."

Frankie knew immediately that Lily knew exactly the favor he wanted to ask and she was not going to make it easy for him.

"My ass was on the line as well, surely you understand?"

"I understand that you will run me over the first chance you get. How is the search for The Ghost coming along?"

"It's the reason I'm calling."

"Oh, you have good news, who is the guy?"

"Come on, Quicksilver, he's a hard man to get a hold of. Throw me a bone, for old times' sake?"

"A bone? A shark with an entire army wants a bone from a solo woman?"

"Jesus, you don't have to rub it in. I'll owe you one."

"What have you got so far?"

"Wind."

Lily was playing with him. At this point, she could give him what he wanted and it would mean nothing. The Scorpion knew who The Ghost was. The assignment was simply a test to know who had the right head on their neck.

"For old times' sake, here is a small clue. He's ex-Shemeji. Surely you can find him after that or do you want me to deliver him to you?"

"Don't mock me. Another thing, let me present this info to The Scorpion, I really need this."

Lily knew how important it was to be owed by a person like Frankie. You never knew when you would need a brute like him on your side.

"Of course, of course. What are friends for?"

CHAPTER 66

Oyunga

OYUNGA HAD JUST touched down from Zanzibar. He was still trying to chew on the contents he had found on the Senator's laptop. At first, he had thought that he was a pervert because the files in his computer were flooded with images of an array of girls, skimpily dressed, all pausing lewdly in different backgrounds.

He looked at the documentation he had taken photos of. Blueprints to buildings in Lavington, Westlands, and Upper Hill. He scanned them with a keen eye but they did not make sense to him. The last documentation made more sense. A permit to a business called Billionaires Club, a big hotel in the heart of Nairobi. It was then that it finally clicked that the Senator was running a brothel. The restaurant was known to attract big names in both the political and entertainment scene. The images of the skimpily dressed girls ran through his head again and he sighed.

He had also come across another piece of information: the images of two high-profile individuals. They were not labeled but Oyunga knew the Governor of Nairobi and the Minister of Energy and Mining when he saw them. He concluded that they were high-flying agents of the cartel. He attached the documents and sent them on encrypted mail to The Ghost.

A message pinged almost immediately. A confirmation of their aliases and positions. The blueprints, well, the Senator owned the building in Westlands, the Governor the one in Lavington, and the Minister of Energy owned the one in Upper Hill.

Oyunga was still trying to wrap his head around the name 'The Black Cat' when his phone buzzed again. It was Arigula. It was incredible how he had become a local sensation almost overnight, and now he wanted a sit-down with Oyunga. 'A quick drink,' is how he put it, as if he didn't understand that Oyunga was a marked man. Not even his celebrity status would protect him from the people he was up against.

His first instinct was to decline but then he felt that he needed to get away from it all and be in a different setting beside the toxic one that he was quickly becoming accustomed to. Had he known what the sit-down with Arigula would snowball towards, he would never have agreed to it.

CHAPTER 67

Arigula

THEY WERE SEATED at a corner of a dainty restaurant. Arigula had picked out the restaurant but Oyunga had picked the corner. It gave him a birds-eye view, allowing him to see who got in and who got out. If he was going to die he wanted to know who pulled the trigger.

Arigula was lolling on his seat, looking at Oyunga with eyes the size of two sunny-side-up eggs. He was fascinated by the idea of chasing a cartel, like a kid getting to play Police and Robber.

Oyunga had thought the meeting would allow him to kick back and have a laugh or two about their bachelor days but Arigula had other ideas. He wanted to know how he was holding up and how he could help.

"You've got to let me in," he said and punched his hand playfully.

"A.G, even sitting with me here right now is a risk for you. You've got too much wild blood; you need someone to keep you grounded."

"Come on, Oyunga, let me be your errand boy. I mean, nobody has use for those."

"You realize this isn't like chasing sunsets with your camera? You could easily end up with a bullet in between your eyes?"

"Wouldn't that heading be glorious, heh? Local Celebrity Gunned Down by Cartel."

"You know they would spin it; the headline would probably read, "Local Celebrity Dies of Pneumonia While Chasing Sundowner on Mt. Kenya.""

"Haha, wouldn't that be something?" He paused. "The life of a celebrated photographer is quite banal. Give me something to kill the time."

"It might kill you instead. I don't think you understand the ramifications." Oyunga let the word 'ramifications' sit on his tongue. It was something he had picked up from The Ghost.

"Ramifications?"

"Yeah, you would need to be in disguise and you'd have to use a different car from your Subaru Outback?" Oyunga said, hoping to make it harder for him and at the same time toying with the idea of using him. He was, after all, short of hands.

"Come on, friend. I'm no fool."

"You've got to be extremely careful."

"Uh-huh, that's my guy."

"Don't make me change my mind."

Oyunga thought for a second. His previous surveillance had gone smoothly. Perhaps too smoothly. He went back to his backpack and removed a file. In it was a crisp, clear photo.

"She's the Minister of Energy and Mining in the country. She currently resides in Kitusuru. These are the plates of her Range Rover. He pushed another photo. I want you to tail her. Tell me where she goes, how long she spends there. I'm especially interested in her hobbies. I haven't found a weakness I can use. Arigula, are you listening?"

Arigula was still in a daze at the beauty of the woman he was staring at.

"Huh, Oyunga, are you giving me an assignment or showing me the love of my life?"

"Please A.G, don't get close to this woman. She sort of has a legend going about her. They call her The Black Cat for a reason. A week is all you have and I'm pulling you off."

"A week is more than enough; you won't regret this."

"Be careful."

Oyunga wanted to take it all back but he knew his friend; he was built in a renegade sort of way. The more you told him to keep off the cookie jar the more he wanted to stick his hand in it. This was probably the best way he could get in this, in a way that Oyunga controlled.

Arigula smiled. He could see the gaping opportunity in this. He could already see himself taking shots of the most notorious drug kingpins in the country. When all this wrapped up he would be somewhat of a legend. It didn't cross his mind even for a second but the moment he took the assignment, the clock on his life started ticking.

CHAPTER 68

Muthoni Page

SHE WAS DRIVEN out of her Kitusuru home in her crimson red Range Rover which was sandwiched between two dark Prados. You could not see her through the tinted black windows but she was seated on the back left of the armored car, next to her *The Art of War* by Sun Tzu.

She was in a light grey skirt suit, a light blue blouse and on her feet, blue high-heels. She did not look her age at all. Her skin was silk-smooth without a single wrinkle. Nobody would argue that she was in her late twenties or early thirties but she was on the edge of forty.

Her beauty was something of a legend. She was often compared in conversation to Helen of Troy and Cleopatra of Egypt. Like Cleopatra, it was said she bathed in donkey milk to keep her skin smooth. And her cunning was like no other. Men lower than her liked to think that she got where she was because of her looks but the smart ones knew better.

Her moniker, The Black Cat, only added to her legend. Besides being agile in how she ran her affairs, it was said that the red carpet she walked on was stained with the blood of dead men. She did not take any chances and if she suspected you even in the slightest way, you would not show up the next day. She earned the name The Black Cat because every time she came out to play something bad was bound to happen.

It was also whispered that Lily was her protégée. That she handpicked her herself and taught her her ways. But those were only whispers.

On record, there was no husband, child, or friend. She was a woman with nothing to nudge at, no strings to pull. Perhaps that is why she had risen to the status of Minister of Energy and Mining and consequently, the Second-in-Command in the Shemeji Cartel.

Her convoy was now pulling up at The Prism Tower in the heart of Upper Hill, Nairobi. Three robust men got out. One opened the door on his left, the other ran ahead, and the third stood as a lookout on the right. On the far edge of the road, he could see a beat-up Toyota IST. He took note of the car. If he saw it a second time, it would be a problem.

Muthoni Page got out of the car and straightened her skirt which fell slightly above her knees so that it was modest. That was another skill of hers. She knew exactly what to wear for every occasion. For this one she needed to appear in control, to show her associates that they were in good hands and that they were making the right move.

Her hair was relaxed, with a pin holding it. It said that she knew her place in this world was below the man. She made a point to refer to The Scorpion now and again so that their new associates would know that this was very much a male operation. She knew that she lived in a society where the female voice, even though sensible, was suffocated by the male voice, even when that voice was full of nonsense, and she played to it.

She started walking and her bodyguards fell around her in a triangle out of habit. The Toyota IST ignited and took off the minute she entered The Prism. The driver of the Range Rover, who also doubled as a bodyguard, followed it with his eyes until it was out of sight.

CHAPTER 69

Arigula

ARIGULA HAD DONE a decent job. He had paid his friend who sold second-hand cars a courtesy visit and borrowed a Toyota IST. He had gone further and gotten a recorder and some knock-off night goggles that made him feel like part of an exclusive SWAT team.

He now sat inside his IST with his telephoto lens which saw nothing more than The Black Cat's Range Rover and the bodyguards manning her. One of whom now had his sticky eye on Arigula's car.

He watched the security detail of The Black Cat from behind his telephoto lens and he now understood why Oyunga told him not to get close. It was impressive. The three bodyguards who escorted her moved as if they were part of her limbs. Two in the front one behind. Walking so that you could never get a real chance to hit her. Not with a round of ammunition nor a camera.

They were all the same height. Slightly taller than her so that you could never tell the weave she was wearing that day or if she was wearing any at all. They formed a perfect triangle, an indestructible pyramid.

Arigula realized that today was not the day he would breach that pyramid. His ambitions had to wait. Immediately Muthoni Page got into her building, he zoomed off. A meeting beckoned. He was a big deal after all. A celebrated local photographer.

CHAPTER 70

Presentation

ARIGULA ALSO DOUBLED as a creative consultant for a young advertising agency. He loved the job. It gave him a window to easy money and easy affairs. He had just done a successful campaign and he was looking forward to gracing the agency with his presence. He loved the praise and even more the eyes that looked at him as if he were a demigod.

He looked at the team of millennials in front of him and smiled, then got glib about how he had to use different outfits on the model to get exactly what he was looking for. He loved to hear the sound of his voice bouncing off the walls. If he could have it his way he would be out on a date with it.

The model in question was a nubile with chocolate skin and a mane of natural hair. He kept telling her something was not right and he couldn't feel the flow when taking her photos but of course, everything became right and he began to feel the flow the moment she agreed to sleep with him.

He was one of those men who wielded his talent as a magic wand to sleep with women. He wondered how many would want to sleep with him if he divulged that he was doing a high-profile project, one involving a sinister drug cartel. He wondered still how many would want to take him to bed after he cracked the case wide open with his lens.

The girl in front particularly piqued his interest. She had been stealing glances at him and averting her eyes whenever he looked in her direction. He had seen her in her full glory when she had gotten up to go to the washrooms. She was in a light brown bubble dress that exposed half her bronze thighs and now she sat there looking at him, her heavy breasts almost spilling out of her brassier.

He finished his presentation and she clapped a bit longer than the rest. It was in that way he handed her his business card and invited her for dinner when she came to congratulate him on his presentation.

CHAPTER 71

The Muscle

"You think the world will miss such a person?"

"Does the world ever miss anybody?"

"I mean you could argue it does. Not the world necessarily, the people you leave behind. They will miss you to an extent until life gets in the way. You know, bills, a date, a kid. And then they will move on."

The Roach rubbed his head as if that was too much information for him to process.

"Think about it, no one is ever remembered for who they are, they are remembered for what they did. Think about someone like that bastard, Michael Jackson. He might have molested little kids but the world remembers him for Thriller. Isn't that a bitch?"

"The world forgets what it wants to forget."

"This asshole, for example. The world will remember him for his photography, not that he was a womanizer, or that he bored people to death with his tedious presentations, which he probably thinks are the next best thing after peanut butter."

"How do you think he will go?"

"He will try to play it cool but this one is a candy-ass. He will beg and defecate himself. He will leave the world the same way he moves on women. With a stench devoid of dignity."

CHAPTER 72

Prisca

PRISCA COULD NOT remember when her life fell apart. She did not know if it fell apart when she married Martin or when her parents cautioned her that he was no good. She did not know if it fell apart the first day Martin laid hands on her, when the sex stopped or when she first saw blood on his clothes. But she was sure something in her tilted that afternoon she came home and Grace was missing.

Martin's schedule had completely changed now. He could go weeks without showing up at the hardware or the house. The afternoon Prisca came and did not find her daughter, she remembered shaking him and hitting him and he was unfeeling, almost like a huge stone.

"Where did you take Grace? Where did you take my child? You killed her, you killed her!"

She was livid. She screamed until her lungs were sore. She had rushed to her phone to call someone, anyone, but one look from Martin and she stopped. She felt he would truly hurt Grace if she called for help.

The loop kept breaking. One minute she was running to the kitchen counter to fetch a knife so she could hurt him. The next she was running towards him with the knife raised in her hand and the next Martin had the knife in his hand and she blacked out.

CHAPTER 73

Premeditated

MARTIN LOCKED HER in the bedroom and whenever he opened the door to give her food she shivered and shrieked and moved back towards the wall. Whispering, she asked, "Where did you take Grace? Where did you take my child? Are you going to kill me like you killed her?"

Prisca's parents would sometimes call to ask how they were doing and the response was the same. "We are trying; you know how she can be sometimes." Their response was also rehearsed. "If you need anything you know you can count on us." He would thank them for calling and the line would go dead.

Sometimes Martin stared at the door to their bedroom and wondered why his parents did not bother calling.

In that gloomy bedroom, Prisca had decided she was going to kill him before he killed her.

She would do it when he came in to bring her food. He was too used to finding her shivering in a corner, afraid. Not this time. She would pounce.

CHAPTER 74

Arigula

ARIGULA SAT WITH his date at the Villa Roma, one of the plushiest hotels in the country. Money could now allow him to splurge on his dates in such flamboyant fashion that could leave an Arab prince in shock.

Laura, his date, had gone out of her way to impress him. She was in a short, purple dress whose waist started below her breasts then fell like a bell just above her knees. She looked as if she had come for a photo-shoot and she crossed her fingers that Arigula would whip out his camera.

She sat with a napkin on her lap, feeding Arigula spiel about how she was working to be a fashion designer. Honestly, he could have done without it. He could have just invited her to his place for a romp but now he had to sit there and listen to her go on and on as if she was the next best thing after Michael Kors and the reincarnation of Coco Chanel.

He was thinking this was a bad investment until he saw The Black Cat. In a pencil skirt and feet that dipped into black stilettos. If you could have put her next to Arigula's date, you could have mistaken Laura for a common maid.

She didn't seem to be in a hurry but her aura had the slightest hint of urgency. Arigula's first impulse was taking his camera out and taking a photo. What came after almost made his ego explode. Muthoni Page got up from her table and walked to his.

"You're that celebrated local photographer," she said giving him her hand. Arigula took it and gave it a warm, gentle kiss.

"I'm surprised you know me," he stammered while getting up.

"What kind of citizen would I be if I didn't know talented artists like you?"

"We should do some work together. You should come to my studio sometime." His studio alternated between photography and love-making on demand.

"How about we do it now?"

"Huh? Now?"

"Yeah. You already have your gear." She pointed at his camera with her manicured forefinger.

"Alright, where?"

"Meet me in room 107 in five and come with your friend."

When Arigula got to room 107 he did not meet Muthoni Page. She had left immediately they rubbed shoulders and she was now in the back left of her Range Rover, filing her nails en-route to The Prism. He met The Roach and Zero. He did scream, only it was in vain because the room was soundproof.

CHAPTER 75

Muthoni Page

IT WAS ALL A COINCIDENCE. Not the tailing part. The Black Cat did not leave anything to chance and she insisted that she be briefed about everything. So when she was told that there was a Toyota IST parked outside The Prism which left when she got into the building, she asked that it be investigated. The plates belonged to a car salesman. On further inquiry, they discovered that it was hired by a local celebrity, Oyunga's friend, and that is how The Roach and Zero found themselves eavesdropping on a presentation.

But the hotel was a coincidence. The Black Cat was there to meet her business associates until she was told Oyunga's friend was in the building as well, on what looked like an innocent date. She did not believe in innocence, or coincidence, or fate. She believed things happened because of choices and decisions and Arigula had made his bed the moment he decided to help Oyunga.

She had made a few phone calls and everything had been arranged. When she walked up to Arigula to say hi and he gleefully invited her for a photo-shoot, she confirmed what she already knew.

This, more than anything, was a message to Oyunga. That the kingpins of the cartel were nothing to play with. If he was alive, it was simply because the cartel wanted it that way.

CHAPTER 76

Oyunga

THE FUNERAL CEREMONY wrapped up quickly as Arigula was Muslim. The burial ceremony was a quiet affair that took less than an hour. There were plans to go back to the bereaved home and say a final farewell, remembering the days he had lived and the accolades he had collected, but Oyunga could not allow himself to attend. He didn't want to stare at long faces or go down memory lane. He felt the guilt would destroy him.

The headline read, 'Romeo and Juliet; Celebrated Photographer Dies in Love Gone Sour.' There was full-blown media coverage on them and discussion panels on what should be done when love is not working. Counselors and relationship gurus were brought on screen and there were entire trending topics on Twitter regarding the circus.

Oyunga knew better. *So much taken and so much to find the thief and no satisfaction, no revenge.* The sentence from Shakespeare echoed in his mind. He had gotten to a point where no tears came out. There was just toxic anger bottled up inside him like poison in a jar, burning both the man and his environment. He blamed himself for all of it without knowing that Arigula had had his agendas.

He looked at the photograph of The Black Cat again and he was filled with questions. He picked up his phone and dialed the first number on his speed dial. It went to voicemail. The Ghost was still at large. Oyunga felt as if he was going round in circles. Perhaps he should also show up at The Prism in a Toyota IST. Having a reunion with Marion and his kids did not feel like such a bad idea.

CHAPTER 77

Compadres

LILY SAT ON the edge of her chair devoid of clothes. A glass of whisky rested on the tips of her fingers. She felt as if her body had been run over by a truck. Her love pocket felt sore. Her skin had pink patches on it. She had loved it at first: the heat of a man close to her, the rush of kissing, and the intensity of undressing and being taken.

She had tried to guide him but his animal side overwhelmed her. He took her from the rear like a dog mounting a bitch. After the third thrust, she had gone dry. He thrust like he was angry at her, as if he was punishing her for something. She had felt aroused again when he yanked her hair and started choking her. The excitement of living and being on the brink of death overwhelmed her and opened up her taps again. But then she dried up when he pinned her down and started drilling.

It was a sort of celebration for him. He had felt like a man for the first time in a long while. He had gotten his fifteen seconds of fame narrating the story of The Ghost and how he was an ex-Shemeji agent. The Scorpion clapped his hands twice and commended him for his brilliant work and sharp mind, and now Frankie kept shouting Fourth-in-Command as he pumped in and out of her.

He finally came in a gush and collapsed on his side of the bed. Lily got up, went to the bedside table, took some tissue, and wiped her womanhood. She went to her bag and got two pills. One was to prevent a pregnancy and the other was to shield her from any sexually transmitted infections.

Frankie breathed heavily.

"That was electric. We're going to take it to the very top, you and I."

"Is that why you kept screaming Fourth-in-Command?"

"Come on, everybody knows the Fourth-in-Command is a finocchio. That is why pretty boy outfoxed him so easily. That position is going to be vacant very soon and thanks to your intel I'm a real contender for it."

Lily smiled. A stone roasting in the sun was a better contender for the position than Frankie. She had slept with him for two reasons. Frankie was like every other man. Immediately he slept with a woman he thought less of her in a way. And she needed him to underestimate her. Also, sex made him blind and he couldn't see past his nose. She needed Frankie to stay blind; it was her best bet to save Oyunga and still have a position in the cartel.

Things were changing. She had tried to sniff The Ghost's trail but it had gone cold. The Ghost was the type of man who hid where you couldn't look and Lily had come to the conclusion that he was after a top-ranking official in the cartel. It couldn't be the fourth, that was too much of an easy picking. The Senator didn't have any power as such, seeing as he loved his women young and his alcohol strong.

That left the third, second, and first. She had also seen documentation that suggested that the cartel was branching out into the larger East Africa region. She brought it up with The Scorpion but he dismissed it, which only confirmed that things were being escalated. Whatever would happen in the next couple of months would shift or shatter the cartel and she needed to make sure she didn't get out of it empty-handed or empty-headed.

She had come to the decision that she would set up Frankie. Why? Because she could. Because she despised his thick skull; anyone with brains could have seen right through that skit by The Scorpion. And because someone had to pay for how sore her pussy felt at that moment.

Some women felt that that was the hallmark of a true lover. Someone who left you sore and unfeeling but that was not her style. Sex, for her, was supposed to be sensual and enjoyable for the people involved.

"We're going to go to the very summit of the cartel," Frankie mouthed huskily while dozing off.

"Of course we are. Of course," Lily rattled like a viper.

CHAPTER 78

Mr. Governor

THE THIRD-IN-COMMAND was your typical rags to riches story. He had been born a single child in a family where the father was a drunkard and the mother was the distiller. Kumi Kumi, the poison was called, and it had reduced him to an orphan.

He had quickly learned to parent himself, scavenging for scrap metal and selling it for money for food. He had gotten into petty crime, snatching a purse, snatching a phone, and removing the side mirror from a parked car. It was while he was trying to sell his stolen goods to one of the local shy-locks that his sharp mind was discovered.

He quickly learned the trade. Lending small money to poverty-stricken families and charging huge amounts of in-terest. If they failed to pay, which was often, he outsourced muscle and took their most valuable assets and sold them for a penny unworthy of their initial cost.

It was in this way that he was able to venture into the matatu business. He soon had a monopoly in Nairobi, Mombasa, and the Central Region, and was now planning to branch out into long-distance travels in East Africa.

He had turned out to be quite the philanthropist in the city: visiting a mother and paying school fees for her kids, buying water for a shanty whose taps had magically gone dry. He had mastered the art of giving a man a fish instead of showing him how to fish and this made him quite a darling among the locals and it was in this way that he was voted in as the Governor of Nairobi and consequently, Third-in-Command to the Shemeji Cartel, his star ever rising.

He now sat in one of his penthouses in Lavington, in a highrise building of seventy-eight floors. Hearsay had it that he had built it from the ground up with taxpayers' money in the short duration of time he had been in office. Rumor also had it that nobody knew the exact floors it had because he kept adding on it. In an interview, he had boasted that it would soon surpass the Burj Khalifa not only in height but in glory as well.

He now sat in his oval office. He was a man of ego and he had constructed his office to resemble that of the ruler of the free world in every sense. He sat in his leather chair anticipating business. The main agenda of discussion was the merger between Dar, Kampala, and Kigali because even crooks loved to diversify and scale-up. The other point of discussion was expanding his transport business into East Africa and finagling the prostitution operation from the Fourth-in-Command. It seemed that everybody in the Shemeji Cartel considered him a weakling.

They arrived, four in number. They were ushered into the oval office by a slender secretary whose hair was held in a ponytail. Two were in black suits, one in grey and the other, dark brown. The ones in black suits represented Kigali. They were tall and fierce. The one in grey was plump and short, he hailed from Kampala. The other one was from Dar. Even in this setting, the associates from Kigali had a bigger voice. Their words were more measured and when they opened their mouths to speak only sense flowed.

The meeting was supposed to be a closely guarded secret but they forgot that there was no secret between two people, much less between five.

"The merger is going down in the first week of next month. I suppose we all know our duties?" the Governor spoke.

"We are aware of this. Even as we speak our people are taking care of the security. Every building adjacent to ours will have our men. It goes without saying that the entire building will be on lockdown for the two hours the meeting will be ongoing," one of the associates from Kigali said.

"Keep the security detail camouflaged. We don't want the top people thinking we're afraid. If we can't run our own turf how will they expect us to run theirs?" the Governor continued.

"Of course, and that's why we are here. Not just as insiders but also as enforcers to make sure everything is watertight." The associate from Kigali spoke with a bit of an accent but before he could look up to see what the response from his associates was, a gaping hole in between the Kampala man's sinuses opened up and sent him sprawling to the floor.

The Kigali associate, still in shock barely mouthed the words, 'What are you doing?' before a round caught him point-blank underneath his jaw, sending his grey matter jutting out from above his ear and splattering on the Dar man's brown suit. The Dar man was now running towards the window. The bullet caught him on his neck and his weight broke the glass, sending him sprawling seventy-eight floors down.

"If it's money you want…" the Governor began. He was not allowed to finish the sentence. The round hit him smack in between his eyes and he fell on the mahogany table, dying the way he had lived. Deviously.

All this happened in less than a minute and before the hue and cry could go up, he was in his car in the basement of the building. He gunned his black sedan out of the gate, removed the mask, and wore the signature hat that covered his face to the base of his nose, and he was a shadow again.

CHAPTER 79

The White Hawk

THE SENATOR WAS the first to arrive, in his jet-black Cadillac Escalade. A bodyguard got out of the front seat and opened the door. The first thing that peeked out were silver, crocodile leather shoes followed by mud-brown trousers, a suit vest, and, on top of it, a long coat. He looked like a pimp in every sense of the word.

Five minutes later, The Black Cat arrived in a black, armored Mercedes Pullman. In front of her there was a Mercedes CLA and behind her a Range Rover Vogue. The convoy came to a halt and three men jumped out of the Range Rover and stood next to the Mercedes Pullman. The door was opened only when The Scorpion arrived in a Rolls-Royce Phantom limousine. Behind him were two Cadillac Escalades and in front of him two official police motorbikes. The limo came to a halt at the foot of the stairs of his 757 private jet.

The jet was dubbed the White Hawk. It was something of a legend in the Shemeji Cartel circles. It was said to have a living room, two master bedrooms, a small golf course, and a conference room that could hold forty people. It was a mansion on wheels and it now stood there in all its glory, its white body and the streaks of black on its wings shimmering in the sun, making it nothing short of a magnificent beast.

Muthoni Page stepped out of her car only after The Scorpion entered the White Hawk. She was in a black side-slit maxi dress and black heels and carried a red clutch bag. Her bodyguards made the usual pyramid around her as she walked into the 757. After she entered, the Senator followed, almost breaking into a small jog. A second after he disappeared into the White Hawk, the doors closed and its five engines roared, breathing like a scorned giant.

The big bird turned, its wheels moving slowly at first, then breaking into a sprint, and in the blink of an eye, it was airborne, the blue and red lights underneath its breasts flick-ering. Not very long after, they were cruising at forty-two thousand feet.

It was a precaution taken after the Third-in-Command was taken out. Meetings between the commanders would now take place in the sky. It was a double-edged statement. It said they had the resources. It also said they considered themselves gods.

The Scorpion sat at the head of the table in the confer-ence room which was styled more like a lounge. Everything in the 757 was adjustable at his request. The Senator was on one side of the white settee and The Black Cat on the other. Her legs were crossed, the slit on her maxi exposing one of them from her heel to her hip. The Scorpion stared at the golden site for a split second before averting his gaze.

"The Ghost has to be taken out before the big meeting," he barked.

"He knows the date the meeting is happening, maybe we can bait him," the Senator followed.

"He's too clever to fall for that. He will expect us to move it. He will expect some things to change," Muthoni Page followed.

"You're right on that. We're going to move the meeting to the end of this month. All protocols will be observed. The security will be doubled. And we will show up as planned. Only we won't be showing up for the meeting, we will be showing up for him."

"How will he get the message?"

It was a stupid question from the Senator. The Ghost had his ways. Immediately Lily and Frankie were briefed it would be as if he was in the briefing room.

The Scorpion groaned and dismissed him. "Our muscle can't know it's a decoy operation. They need to think it's very much the big event we have been anticipating. That way The Ghost can show his head and hopefully Oyunga too and we can snap them once and for all."

The Black Cat shifted her weight from one leg to the other and took a glass of water. Her face was unreadable.

"And Senator, please get your act together. We can't have another one of our top officials taken out the same way you would swat a fly. Increase your security detail… ten times if you must. I hope I won't have to repeat myself."

It sounded nonchalant but that was The Scorpion scolding him. Telling him in not so many words that he needed to style up or his position and his life would be in jeopardy. He nodded his head in agreement.

The White Hawk had turned and it was now dipping. It

approached the runway and its feet kissed it the same way a mother kisses her child, slightly and lovingly, before coming to a halt next to The Scorpion's limo. He entered the limo hurriedly and left. The same pyramid of bodyguards escorted Muthoni Page to her Pullman and it gunned off while the Senator struggled with something in his shoe at the entrance of the plane.

CHAPTER 80

Oyunga

"You're going to be the getaway," The Ghost said from behind his hat. Oyunga had, of course, seen him without it but
he was starting to forget. Whenever he thought of something sinister, something beyond grasp, The Ghost and his
hat often came to his mind. He shifted in his seat, tapped a
cigarette out of a packet, and put it afire.

"It's all planned then, in the basement?"

"Yes, I want you in the capacity of driver and driver
only. No monkey business on this one."

"Monkey business, come on, you've got to give me more
credit than that."

"It's too risky. There will be too many moving pieces
and you can't be caught in the middle of it."

"I'm a big boy, I can take care of myself."

"The biggest piece of the puzzle right now is The Scorpion. The others are inconsequential, at least for now."

"I won't be in your way with The Scorpion but let me at least get Lily."

"You don't understand. This is bigger than a vendetta. I mean, I am sad that the mother of your kids got involved. But this is bigger than her."

Oyunga's brow furrowed and his physique tensed. They were seated on the rooftop of a beat down hotel in downtown Nairobi. Oyunga smashed his cigarette on the dirty ashtray. He was having a hard time understanding when this operation stopped being his and become that of The Ghost.

"You're the one who has it misunderstood, old man. This operation is mine," he said with a bang of his fist on the table, making the contents on it go airborne for a split second. Deep in his gut, he knew this operation wasn't his. In any case, if it wasn't for The Ghost his body would be entertaining worms, six feet below the ground.

"I thought we discussed this? The Scorpion is the key to all this. Immediately he's taken care of, the rest will unravel like a single thread from the seam, bringing the entire fabric undone." He paused and tipped his hat. "But you need to brace yourself for the possibility of working with your enemies. Your enemies are standing at a vantage point and they might help you more than you want to imagine."

Instinctively, Oyunga knew he was talking about Lily. He was wondering what kind of animal would expect him to crawl into the same bed sheets with the one person that kept him awake at night.

"I don't know which team you are playing for but whichever team it is, it's not mine," he said, took his jacket from the armrest of his chair, and disappeared behind the portico.

The Ghost tipped his hat so it almost covered his entire nose. He knew Oyunga would come to his senses after he got some air. He just hoped it would be sooner rather than later because the big event was on the door knocking.

CHAPTER 81

The Brief

"To think you wanted to be the Fourth-in-Command and now you have a real shot at third, huh, Frankie?" Lily said with a smile.

"Careful, some things are said as japes but then end up being true. Let me think what my first order of business will be as Third-in-Command. I think it will be taking out your loverboy if he is lucky enough to have stayed alive that long."

"Surely the Third-in-Command will have more important business than handling my lovers?"

"Yes, bedding his newlywed, for example," he said, breathing in Lily's lustrous hair. For a moment she let him, before backing away two steps.

"We need to focus on this. If something goes wrong we are dead meat."

On the table were bulletproof vests, one M14, two M16s, and a couple of pistols. They were loading the guns' magazines and adorning the pistols with silencers. The blueprint to The Prism was blown up on a screen adjacent the table. They had circled all the potential places The Ghost might think of entering from. This time he would not catch them unawares.

They had the advantage of knowing that his long arm did not know the kingpins of Kigali, Dar nor Kampala. He had left the cartel a long time ago and this was a very new operation, two years in the making. But with The Ghost, you could never be too sure.

His best shot would be to get The Scorpion once he alighted or after the meeting. But that was uncertain. After he alighted and after the meeting, there would be too much movement and movement meant margins of error. The Ghost was not a man who sat and dined at the same table with margins of error.

The other possibility was that he would be in disguise as one of the waiters. All of them had been vetted and cleared. They would be searched further before they entered the conference room. The slightest mistrust and a sniper on the roof would take any one of them out without hesitation.

They went through the brief again. The Senator would arrive, followed by the Minister of Energy and Mining, then the Vice President. Following swiftly would be the three principals. All the guards had to be out of sight because as much as possible, the principals had to see for themselves that things were under control.

But something about this brief didn't sound right to Lily. It was too simplistic. It wasn't the Shemeji Cartel style at all. There was no tour, there wasn't an after-party. It was like a decoy prepared to bait a single person. She prepared her mind for anything. It was also during these thoughts that she came up with a plan to set up Frankie.

CHAPTER 82

Operation Mongoose

THEY ALL ARRIVED the way they had planned it. The Senator was the first to arrive in his black Cadillac Escalade. Behind it was a Prado V8 and in front of it a Range Rover House. A guard got out of the Range Rover and opened the Cadillac's back left door. The Senator was in a formal suit. His hair cut military style. He disappeared into The Prism.

Muthoni Page showed up in a trouser suit and wedge heels. She was dressed in a way that would allow her to sprint if she needed to. This time she did not have her usual pyramid. Her driver opened her door and she disappeared into the building. Then followed The Scorpion. There were two guards dressed like simple servants, one before him and one behind him. One got into the lift with him and disappeared after he entered the conference room.

The three principals from Kigali, Dar, and Kampala followed in a Mercedes E-Class, a Volkswagen Toureg, and a Hummer respectively.

After they were all settled in, Oyunga got out of a black sedan in the basement of the building. The sedan was a Shemeji Cartel car and the agent lay dead in the boot courtesy of The Ghost. They had agreed they would use the car as a getaway but they had not agreed on Oyunga getting out of the car. He got out and closed the door. He had his own vendetta.

Frankie was the one who saw him. He waited until Oyunga disappeared and went to the car. The door was not locked. Immediately, he realized it was the getaway car; the keys inside the visor only confirmed that. He thought for a second. Should he raise the alarm? No, he did not want them to know that Oyunga and possibly The Ghost were in the building. He wanted all the glory to himself. He wired the car with C4. It would go off immediately the engine woke up. He smiled at his wits and walked away whistling.

The six waited for fifteen minutes. There was no movement. Everything was silent.

"You don't suppose our friend got word about our meeting, do you?" The Scorpion whispered to The Black Cat.

"Everything has been quiet."

"Word from informers?"

"They have been around our other friends. Everything has been brick-silent."

The Senator moved uneasily on his seat, knowing the word 'friends' loosely meant people in the cartel who couldn't be trusted. People like him.

"I don't like this one bit. Call it off after I leave," The Scorpion said. This would have been Frankie's moment to call it in but he didn't. Instead, he called The Scorpion's body-guard who got into the lift and ushered The Scorpion in.

It was on the thirtieth floor that the lift came to a halt. The roof opened and in a split second the guard dressed as a servant lay dead on the floor. It was not The Ghost's intention to kill The Scorpion. He meant to have a chat with him. Know how far and deep the cartel's roots ran. After, maybe he would let him live. Maybe he wouldn't.

The lift opened in the basement. He quickly took out the other guard and the two agents stationed at the door. He knocked The Scorpion unconscious and threw him in the backseat of the getaway car while wondering where the hell Oyunga was. He counted on The Scorpion's army follow-ing him with everything they had to be distraction enough for Oyunga to get away. But immediately he stepped on the gas and turned the ignition, everything went pitch black. A whirring sound hit fever pitch as the car was blown to bits of metal, blood, and grey matter.

CHAPTER 83

The Couple

THE EXPLOSION GOT Frankie back to the fray. He felt as if he was seeing a ghost. Oyunga was running towards the explosion, a deja vu of sorts for him. Lily was hot on his heels. "Stop, stop, it's a setup!" she was screaming. She was counting on Frankie to wire the getaway car and take all the glory but she didn't know if he had other surprises in store and if Oyunga was walking into a landmine.

Frankie pulled the hammer back on his Glock 19 semi-automatic pistol and aimed it at Oyunga. The first shot made him lose his balance, the second one sent him tumbling down like a bag of bricks. Lily swooped in and placed his right arm on her left shoulder, her adrenaline kicking in at full speed. She dragged him towards the Jeep Wrangler she had planned to get away with.

Frankie aimed his Glock for a third but Lily was in the way. The lack of doors and a roof on the Jeep made it easier for her to push Oyunga onto the passenger seat. His head rested on her laps as she turned on the ignition and gunned the car towards the exit. Frankie stood smack in the middle of the driveway, his Glock 19 aimed point-blank at Lily's face.

"I swear to God, step out of the car or I will drop you to the ground."

Lily stepped on the gas and Frankie jumped out of her way. He still couldn't pull the trigger even though she was trying to do everything to save a man he despised. In his peculiar way, he did care about her. The woman who had just set him up.

CHAPTER 84

Muthoni Page

ON THE FORTY-THIRD FLOOR, the Second-in-Command turned on the sensors to the lifts and the surveillance cameras to the building. She then marched to the table and mixed herself a drink. Two fingers of Jack Daniels and a half a finger of Sprite. Her plan had gone swimmingly. She was fascinated by how well Lily knew Oyunga and Frankie. That hot-headed guy could never have stayed in that car and the muscle, he would have always wanted all the glory to himself. Third-in-Command, huh? She smiled at how badly people misread situations.

And The Ghost. He was getting rusty. He had become predictable. She always knew that his play would be the lifts. He was a sacrifice that had to be made. The Ghost could have never turned but Oyunga, he was still young and green. With the right story and the right storyteller, he could be turned.

She felt a bit lightheaded after her first shot of whiskey, as if she could break down any minute, but then decided she would do it in private, away from prying eyes.

She picked her drink and proceeded to the big, glass window and stared at her men running frantic, cleaning the mess that had ensued below her heels. The Senator was behind her, following her, not only with his body but also with his spirit. The man was smarter than people had given him credit for.

"The whole East Africa is now at your feet, how do you feel?"

She didn't hear a word the Senator said. She had other images in her mind. Images of a more nurturing kind. Images of things that had occurred more than two decades ago. Oyunga running around with a football as a toddler, The Ghost running after him and snatching away the ball. Oyunga shouting, 'Daddy, daddy.' She shed a single, cold tear and then wiped it off as if she had something in her eye. She had a cartel to run.

EPILOGUE

Prisca

MARTIN CAME IN to bring Prisca food before he left for work as usual. He did not see her in her usual spot. He thought that maybe she was hiding in the bathroom but before he could make another step something jumped on his back from behind. It was frail and weak and paper-weight; it was his wife.

She did not manage to push him two steps before he wrung free.

"Where did you take Grace? Where did you take my child? Are you going to kill me like you killed her?"

Her voice was hoarse and strained. Martin started moving back, the food he had carried had splattered all over the floor. He moved another step and slipped on the wet floor, his head hitting the adjacent wall with a thud.

When their parents and the ambulance came, Prisca was still murmuring, "Where did you take Grace? Where did you take my child? Are you going to kill me like you killed her?"

Her parents looked at her with sad faces. Grace had died a few months after birth from a respiratory infection. It was Martin who noticed the cough. They took Grace to the hospital and she was given a syrup. They woke up the next morning to find her cold and unmoving, with her big brown eyes wide open, and Prisca was never the same.

"He needs to be punished!" Prisca screeched as the paramedics pushed her husband on a wheeled stretcher into the ambulance. She tried to scream but it came out as a whisper, "He needs to be punished." The doors to her dad's Volvo closed and they sped towards Chiromo Mental Hospital.

Acknowledgments
To my sisters
Wambui
Nyambura
Gathoni
and Shiku
for being a constant source of love and inspiration.
This one is for you.

About the Author

Kariuki Kimuyu is a writer based in Nairobi. He graduated from Strathmore University with a Bachelor of Commerce, majoring in Management Science (because he had to major in something).

He has tried his hand at advertising, working in mainstream and digital media for over four years, but soon quit to pursue his true north.

He hopes his writing gains enough notoriety for his parents to be able to explain to their friends what their son does for a living. He also hopes they stop asking him when he is 'bringing someone home.'

He is currently working on his first poetry collection and the sequel to Drug Paradise, 'The Black Cat.' When he is not whacking away at the keyboard you can find him taking long walks or stopping to buy anything consumable on the roadside.

Read him on: www.kisauti.com

Or catch up with him on his social pages, @wakimuyu on Instagram, Facebook, and Twitter.

K. Kimuyu

KESHO & MALKIA

Divided by Misfortune, Brought Together by Blood

Turn page to read preview...

1.

Kesho

KESHO WAS OUTSIDE Nation Centre foraging through trash, in oversized purple shorts and a torn t-shirt that exposed him from left nipple to ribs. Ribs that you could count one by one like withered sticks. The t-shirt had been white a long time ago but now it was brown with dark oil spots.

His purple shorts were cleaner but they were baggy, meant for a man, not a boy. They were fastened with a string to keep from falling. He had picked them from *Gikomba* earlier in the morning while they opened fresh bales of second-hand clothes.

The vendors did not notice as he squeezed and turned and came out with purple shorts. He would have come out with more but he had learned to be cautious. He had seen more than one man get stoned to death for stealing something as small as a purse, a purse that had less than five shillings in it.

He rummaged through the trash cans outside Nation Centre. On a bad day, he found nothing, on a good one he found bottles that he traded in for some money for food, on a great day he found leftover Kentucky Fried Chicken from the uppity of Nairobi who had had their fill and thrown the rest for the dogs. Today was not just a bad day; it was worse. Not only was there nothing of value in the bin, but the watchman also had a sticky eye on him.

"Chokora nilikuambia nisiwahi kuona hapa tena." A thin, dark man in blue uniform pointed a fat rungu at him.

He did not flinch; he was used to the empty threats. But then the watchman started inching towards him then broke into a jog, and that's when Kesho realized things were serious. He started running. The string on his purple shorts came undone and he had to either hold them by the waist or leave them behind.

He ran across the road while holding his waist, jumped across cabbages being sold on the pavement, squeezed in between two matatus, passed through an alley, and lost the guard, but he knew he would be seeing him again. Nation Centre was his prime spot. It was a mecca for restaurant-goers and he almost always found food or bottles to sell. The problem with too many restaurants was too many guards, and they had marked him.

"Nisione hawa chokora hapa. Wanatuharibia biashara," he had heard men in suits tell the guards not once.

He sat at his corner with a somber face. Today he would have to sleep hungry. He hated it when his stomach was empty. Sleep did not come easy and he had to stay up for long hours courting it, flirting with it to take him but all he felt was the rumbling of his stomach, the buzzing of mosquitos, the hooting of cars, and the high heels of hookers hitting the pavement or the crescendo of their voices fighting for clients.

2.

Malkia

Malkia usually opened her business at midnight. That's when her clients got bold enough to come out and play. Sometimes they needed a stiff drink or two to give them the courage, other times they needed the dark of night to give them the push to act according to the needs of their burning loins.

She usually passed via Sonford Fish & Chips and bought a bag of fries and a quarter chicken. Today she was running late and decided to eat on the street.

She made to throw away the bag after she was done. A body in the corner of the street stirred. Brown eyes burnt like a torch in the dim light. The rest of the body was hidden in a dirty blanket and a worn-out suitcase.

"Usitupe," a small boy's voice hummed.

He could not be any older than fifteen, Malkia thought and felt pity. "Zimebaki chipo tatu na mifupa."

"Nipee, ziko sawa hivo."

Malkia inched closer and squatted next to the boy, her micro-mini skirt peeling up her thighs to the size of a belt. She gave him the bag and proceeded to watch him clear the fries and clean the scanty meat on the bones. His teeth continued to dig into them, turning them to shreds.

"Asante."

"Karibu," she said, wanting to break into tears.

She got up, smoothed her skirt, and started back to her group.

"Malkia, nani anakusumbua?" Kavengi asked loudly in between smoke rings.

"Ah, ni chokora tu."

"Ni ule pale, tumfunze adabu saa hii?"

"Wachana na yeye hana story."

Malkia took the cigarette Kavengi was smoking, gave it three puffs, and returned it to her. "Hawa chokora wamekua wengi sana," Kavengi continued absentmindedly. Daniela gave Malkia a mint to clear the cigarette smell and Lisa gave her lip gloss after she was done applying her lipstick.

They had all hated her when she first came to the street. She was younger and more comely than all of them so they had been fiercely jealous of her. "Wewe malaya unaringa na kuma ni ile ile?"

Kavengi, who was tall with masculine features that not even tiny skirts and silk could make feminine, had fought her on the fourth night on the street, after Malkia took her biggest client the night before. "Ntakuharibu hii sura tu-one ni mwanaume mgani atakutaka," Kavengi had said. She had kicked, slapped, punched, and scratched Malkia's face, bloodying it and leaving bruises that took almost three months to heal. But even that did not keep her from coming back to the streets, and even with her swollen face men often preferred her to the others.

"Wewe Malaya, hio kuma yako umeweka nini, juju? Tutakuja na makasi tukurarue hadi kwa tumbo," Daniela had yelled in frustration one night.

"Hata ukirarua hadi kwa mdomo wanaume watanichagua wakuache hapo tu," Malkia had fired back.

Kavengi had snorted out a loud laugh, followed by Lisa, and soon they were all laughing and that's how their camaraderie began.

Malkia closed the lip-gloss lid and returned it to Lisa then looked at the boy in the corner, now fast asleep, and the sadness gripped her again. She wondered about the misfortunes he might have had. She thought about him going all day without food and her eyes became glassy. She blinked the tears away and decided she would be sharing her dinner with him and maybe they would also build a camaraderie of their own.

3.

The Clients

AFTER KESHO WENT to sleep, Malkia's job started. A fat, graying man with a bald head and a colorful suit held her by the hand and took her behind the alley. His maroon pants dropped down together with Malkia's knees. They were there for three minutes before Malkia came back out, wiping the dirt on her knees and the white on her mouth and counting her money while she gargled a mouthful of mouthwash and then spat it out.

A young gent came along. He had the demeanor of a teenager but Malkia knew he was a man grown. They disappeared into a nearby lodging. After twenty minutes she came out counting her money, touching up her makeup and gargling her mouthwash.

Two girls came staggering into the streets. They were new in town, looking for fun. They took her hand and they disappeared into the same lodging.

Malkia always found girls fun and harmless. Besides, kissing and finger-fucking wouldn't keep you out of a job after nine months. After an hour, Malkia came back out counting her money, touching up her makeup, and gargling her mouthwash.

The hour hand sat at 3. She had made good money tonight but she decided she would take one more client before heading home. She had barely finished the thought when a Toyota Sientra flashed its lights and she ran towards it. In the back seat was a gent. He appeared to be in his mid-forties. He opened the door and Malkia got in.

"What's the fee?"

"Depends on the service you want."

"I want the remainder of your night."

"Ten thousand bob," Malkia said, clenching her fist and looking at the gent to see if he thought she had overpriced. It was like any other commodity—negotiable—and she would have gone as low as three thousand bob, but she thought she was having such a great night, why not close it with a bang?

The gent nodded. She thanked her lucky stars and looked outside the window. She did not want the gent to see how pleased she was. She was pleased even more when she realized the car was pulling into a five-star hotel. *Finally, a break from alleys and dingy lodgings.*

They had a hearty dinner, quiet, besides the clinking of cutlery, before heading to the gent's lavish room. Malkia started undressing but he did not want sex, he just wanted to cuddle and listen.

"I am sterile, you know. I can't get it up," he mouthed, the words sticking in his throat for a split second.

"So how do you have any fun?"

"I listen and I touch. I am a great toucher."

"And kids?"

"None."

"What do your parents say?"

"My parents think I'm selfish, avoiding the responsibility of a wife and kids."

"A wife you can get. This world is vast and it caters to everybody and their shortcomings."

The guy smiled. "Enough about me. What about you, what do your parents think about your trade?"

"I don't have parents," she said with a flat voice.

"What about siblings?"

"Not that I know of."

"I'm sorry."

"Don't be. You can't be sad about things you have never experienced."

They cuddled and Malkia talked and talked. She almost thought his ears would fall off but he listened until there was no more talk left and they fell asleep.

Malkia woke up the following morning and the gent was not beside her. She thought perhaps he had gone to have breakfast at the hotel restaurant. She toyed with the idea of joining him but decided she wasn't in a talking mood. She ordered room service, wiped her breakfast clean, and jumped in the shower.

After the shower, the gent was still nowhere to be seen. She opened drawers and looked under things but he had not left her fee. The most she found was a picture of him next to a woman and three smiling kids who looked like carbon copies of him. *Why lie?* she wondered. But most men were like that. They loved being men they were not. She just wondered why he had to be sterile.

She dressed, touched up her makeup, and went to the

front office desk where she was met by a smiling receptionist. The smile was less cordial and more knowing.

"Oh, room 302, John? He checked out."

"Did he leave any cash for his companion?"

She smiled again. "Companion? Not really, no. He was here on business. His bill was already paid for by the company." The receptionist typed on the computer then gave her a receipt. "Here is your bill."

The blood drained from Malkia's face. She took the receipt, ready to raise hell. But then all that was there was the supper and breakfast that she had eaten, totaling to eight thousand bob. All the money she had made for the night. She paid, annoyed.

"I hope you enjoyed your stay enough to come back again," the receptionist said, flashing her knowing smile.

4.

Kesho

Kesho was woken up by the opening of doors, cleaning of floors, cold water seeping into his worn-out suitcase, and the hooting of cars. He got up, folded his dirty blanket, and threw it into the wet suitcase. He then got his gum and sniffed it. It helped kill the pangs of hunger, if only for a bit.

He jumped out of the way before a matatu hit him. "Wewe chokora angalia kwenye unaenda!" He proceeded towards Gikomba. Sometimes he got some work ferrying sacks of potatoes, tomatoes, or bales of clothes from one point to another and got a plate of hot food or some money to buy a meal. But today he was getting sneers and clicks and eyes that told him that he was not welcome.

"Wewe chokora hiyo kinyasa uliiba wapi?" a vendor chirped as he passed.

"Hakuna kazi ya chokora hapa," another one roared.

Someone pinched their nose with their thumb and fore-finger as he passed by.

"Unataka kazi? Enda uongee na Jonte, ule chali mre-fu mnono. Mwambie ni Timo amekutuma," a dirty guy with clever eyes told him as he bit into a mandazi that he was holding with a nylon paper.

"Unataka nini hapa?"

"Nimetumwa na Timo. Amenishow uko na job."

"Kuja nikushow."

He was taken to the public toilets around the corner and given a tin bucket with a string. Flies buzzed everywhere and even Kesho couldn't help pinching his nose with his thumb and forefinger.

"Umewaifanya kazi ya honey sucker?" Jonte asked. Kesho shook his head sideways. "Usijali, haina kisomo. Unaingisha hii mkebe ndani, unachota asali, alafu unamwaga kwa ile drum iko kwa mkokoteni. Timo ataenda kuimwaga Nairobi River masaa yake, umeshika?"

Kesho nodded. "Na pesa?"

"Tutaongea ukimaliza."

Kesho stunk rotten when he was done. He smelled like a manhole and his purple shorts were covered in shit stains. He looked for Jonte for more than two hours but he was nowhere to be found.

"Wewe chokora enda ukaoge."

"Ati Jonte? Kamtafute kwa bafu."

Darkness was almost falling when he decided to head back. He could not trace Jonte or Timo, so he figured he would go rummage through Nation Centre's trash cans for bottles or something to eat or both, and look for them on the morrow.

He got to Nation Centre at around 10:00 pm and found

a bottle of half-drunk passion juice and a half-eaten sandwich full of ants in one of the bins. He brushed the ants away, gobbled down the sandwich in one bite, and washed it down with passion. He then found three empty water bottles, an empty soda can, and two empty plastic dishes from takeaway food. He was putting them in his torn suitcase and then he was running while holding his purple shorts full of shit stains to keep them from falling.

"Wewe chokora nitakuambia mara ngapi sitaki kukuona hapa?" The thin guard with a fat rungu was hot on his heels. Kesho jumped over a pothole, entered a deserted alley, squeezed between two parked minibuses, and lost the guard.

He got to his corner as it was approaching midnight. He opened his worn-out suitcase, removed his rag of a blanket, and made his bed. He cozied up. His stomach was still complaining. It would have to wait till the morrow when he sold his plastics or got his money from Jonte. He was almost nodding off to sleep when someone blocked his light. It was the lady from the night before in her high heels. Her arm was bruised and her left eye was dark and swelling. In her hands was a paper bag that smelled like a hot meal. Kesho looked at her with warm eyes and smiled for the first time that day.

5.

Malkia

WHEN KESHO WAS being chased by guards, Malkia had already gotten to her spot. She was low on cash. She had not even bought her usual packet of chicken and fries. She had decided to open her business early, and with luck, get three to four clients and be sorted for the week.

"Leo umekuja mapema, eh? Economy mbaya," Kavengi barked with a smile, impressed with her quip.

"Umekuja mapema hata boyfriend yako hajafika bado," Daniela laughed.

"Wacheni mchezo, si ule ni client?" Lisa sang inquiringly.

A black Isuzu D-Max was slowing down on their street. The window rolled down and Kavengi ran towards the car. "Call the one in the short, pink skirt," Kavengi made the walk of shame back and called Malkia.

The client was of average height, chocolate-skinned, and toned like he exercised or frequented the gym. He was decently dressed in black jeans, a simple white t-shirt, and sneakers. He had a menacing feel to him. Malkia could always read the occupation of her clients but for some reason, she could not place this one. Was he a producer, a manager, an expatriate?

Malkia clicked her safety belt as her head buzzed. She glanced at the client and another thought crossed her mind, *You could have a decent girlfriend, why are you picking up a prostitute?* She tucked the question away. Asking such questions was how an imbecile got herself out of a paycheck. And besides, men were peculiar. Even men with extremely beautiful wives found themselves in these same streets paying for her services.

"What's your name?" An authoritative voice came out of the client's mouth.

"My name is Malkia."

"Malkia, are you ready to have fun tonight?"

Malkia pondered the question for a minute. Fun could mean anything. "Yes, I'm ready to show you a good time," she said confidently. She found that men loved a coy girl, and when she was bold and took charge, their manhood recoiled. She loved it that way. It was the easiest way to make a buck.

"And how much are you going to charge me for this good time?"

"Five thousand bob only," she said quickly, trying not to push her luck. Saying 'only' immediately made her feel cheap but she was usually cheaper.

"That's a lot of money for a piece of flesh. I hope you will make it worth my while."

A piece of flesh? Malkia thought, irritated. *Maybe you should go get it from a dog or a sheep then.* She thought of unbuckling her seatbelt and getting out of the car, but instead, her shaky voice rasped, "I will."

The D-Max engine roared and in less than half an hour they pulled into a silent, upper-class neighborhood. The kind where everybody minds their business, doors are locked and you seldom know your neighbor. A guard opened the gate, the client parked the car, and they were soon in his sixth-floor apartment.

She looked at the apartment. It was well kept, modest with a hint of luxury. She wondered if the client had rented it just for trysts, or if the wife was out of town. She looked at her client and wondered if he was a bachelor or if his family was back in the village. She could not put a finger on either.

She found men who brought her to apartments generous but entitled. They usually demanded her entire night. She removed her heels and stepped on the clean, crisp carpet, and decided she would negotiate her fee if her client became greedy with her time.

"Will you eat? There is food in the microwave."

She gobbled down goat ribs and rice as the client took a shower.

"There is a fresh towel if you want to take a shower too."

Malkia realized that it was not a request but a command, and she headed towards the bathroom. Besides, she needed a shower.

They started kissing after she dried herself up. Most clients considered her dirty and they just wanted to get done with the act quickly, but not this one. He frenched her and then went down on her. Malkia moaned and groaned. The client got back up for air with his manhood stiff in his hand, ready to get his money's worth.

"Please put on a condom." She reached for her handbag. She always carried protection, just in case.

"It's not sweet with rubber," he spoke softly, his voice heavy.

"No, we can't. Wrap up or back up."

He went to his drawer and came back with a wad of notes which he threw at her. "There, that's double your fee." She took the money and put it in her purse. "Now give me what I want or we're going to have a problem."

"No rubber, no fun." Malkia was relentless.

His slap was quick. Malkia did not see it coming and it sent her to the headboard of the bed.

"I feed you, clean you, and pay you and you still refuse me?" Another quick slap touched her left cheek and she fell off the bed.

"Look what you made me do. Now I'm going to take what's mine by force."

He took her by the arm and threw her back on the bed. Malkia struggled as he pinned her by her waist and parted her legs. She wrenched free momentarily and managed to kick his stomach with her right leg.

"Help! Help!" she screamed.

"Come back here, you stupid whore. Nobody can hear you."

Before she could scream again a big hand covered her mouth. She bit into it with all the strength her jaws could muster and he let go. The next thing she felt was a punch on her left eye. She got dizzy. For a second, her world spun and became blurry.

In her bag were pepper spray and a penknife. She tried desperately to reach for it. The client held her by her right leg. She wrenched free again and kicked him on the arm with her left foot. Anticipating another punch, she moved to the side where her bag was and the punch found the mattress.

"You think you're clever but you're just a stupid whore."

He gripped her left leg with all his strength, pulled her towards himself, and made to get on top of her. The pepper spray caught him unawares. While he rubbed it off his eyes, Malkia stuck the penknife deep in his leg. She took her bag, clothes, and shoes, and opened the door using the keys that were on the table, then ran for dear life. The watchman could not stop a naked woman from getting out of the gate.

It was midnight when she got to the city center. She thought of going back to her house, then with a grin, she decided that today was her lucky night. She had just made ten thousand bob, why not make more? She made for her corner but stopped momentarily as if she had remembered something, then headed towards Sonford Fish & Chips.